BOARDWALK REIGN

JILLIAN FROST

BOARDWALK REIGN

JILLIAN FROST

BOARDWALK REIGN

JILLIAN FROST

Epigraph

"You can do anything, but never go against the family."

~ *The Godfather*

Chapter One

ANGELO

I didn't have a good feeling about this meeting. It was too sudden, sprung on us last minute by Paulie and the Vitales. My brothers agreed that Dad was not acting like himself.

Not acting like the boss.

Paulie was making all the decisions for our family and adding our dad's stamp of approval. Dad had forgotten a lot of shit lately, and Paulie was taking advantage of my old man's age.

I didn't fucking like it.

We gathered at Monviso, an Italian restaurant in the city owned by a family friend. This was neutral territory, making it the perfect place to meet.

The master manipulator entered the dining room with a plate of antipasto. Paulie set it on the table and slid into the leather booth beside my father. Dante was on his right, glaring at Paulie. He had been suspicious of him for a long time, especially after Nico informed our father of his advisor's movements.

Paulie was taking unauthorized meetings on our family's behalf. We went to our dad with our concerns, but he brushed them off. He said we were overreacting.

After his oldest friend betrayed him, I would have thought he would wise up. See that the people around him were snakes.

I reached for a piece of crusty bread and bumped into my twin's arm. He shoved me, so I tapped Stefan's hand and took the bread from him. Most people thought I was older than Stefan because he always let me get my way. But he was older by two minutes and never let me forget it.

Paulie propped his elbow on the table and glanced at us. "Vincenzo is amenable to negotiation. I think we can come to an arrangement that benefits both families."

"Agreed." Dad sipped from his glass, eyeing his advisor from beneath his dark brows. "The marriage between Dante and Vittoria is a much better solution to a war."

What the fuck?

He made simple mistakes like this all the time. Stefan shook his head. We were all worried about him.

"You mean Ava, Papa," I said to correct his mistake.

"Huh?" His head snapped to me. "Didn't I say that?"

Dad's eyebrows knitted together in confusion. He wore the same look often.

It fucking killed me to see the great Salvatore Luciano losing his shit. My dad was a legend in Atlantic City. One of the most feared Mafia bosses in history. And yet, he was nothing like the man people whispered about in the streets.

The man everyone respected.

"No." I sighed. "You said Vittoria."

The Vitales had been our rivals since before my birth. But, for some reason, Dad wasn't interested in feuding with the Atlantic City crime families.

It didn't make sense.

Paulie touched my dad's arm to reassure him. "It's okay, Sal. I'll handle the negotiations."

Of course, he would.

He'd make another deal behind our backs and fuck all of us. I didn't trust Paulie as far as I could throw him.

Dante stirred beside me, shoving up his jacket sleeve to check the time. He had a thing about people respecting his time. That much he'd made clear with

Ava repeatedly over the past few months of her working for us.

She was home with Nico, hanging out at his place until we returned. Someone had to stay with her. We didn't trust our enemies not to steal her from us.

Stefan leaned closer to speak in my ear. "The Vitales are late."

Five minutes to be exact.

"I got a bad feeling, Lo."

I shrugged against the bench and lowered my voice. "They could've gotten stuck in traffic."

Dante balled his hand into a fist on the table, gritting his teeth. The mood in the room shifted to dangerous territory within minutes. By not showing, the Vitales were intentionally disrespecting us.

I downed another glass of scotch while Stefan played a game on his phone. He was so easily distracted and got bored quickly.

"I'm done waiting," Dad said, his voice deep and dripping with anger. "No more negotiations."

The front door swung open, slamming into the wall. A group of men in suits stormed into the dining room, bandanas covering most of their faces.

I attempted to get up but couldn't move with Paulie at the end, trapping us in the booth. "What the fuck?"

Quicker than the rest of us, Dante reached for the gun holstered to his chest. I grabbed mine, and so did

Stefan. A bullet hit Dante in the chest before he could fire the weapon.

"Paulie, move!" Dad shouted.

His advisor held his ground, not even bothering to arm himself. So my brothers and I shot at the men. One bullet hit Dad in the shoulder, another one in the chest.

I flipped up the table with Stefan's help and used it to shield ourselves. But it was wood, and with our attackers shooting at close range, it was impossible not to get hit. A bullet went straight through the table and hit my arm. A searing pain spread through my body.

Stefan took one in the left arm. He winced, breathing harder.

"Fuck," he hissed.

Dante fired a round before he ran out of ammo. I held my gun above the table, even though it hurt like fucking hell to raise my arm, and pulled the trigger until I emptied the chamber. Bullets sailed past Dante's head and burrowed into the leather booth.

To my right, Dad clutched his chest. Dante put his hand on his shoulder. He was breathing harder than usual, blood staining his white dress shirt. His head fell back against the booth, his eyelids fluttering. I felt his pain, which was almost unbearable. Two shots hit me, one in the arm, another in my chest.

Dante blinked rapidly, his bloody fingers spreading over the wound. His blood dripped onto the bench.

Paulie wasn't in the booth with us, but I heard his voice from a distance. "I told you they would fall for it."

Using every bit of my strength, I forced my eyes to stay open. I lifted my head to look through one of the bullet holes in the table.

"Thanks for helping us out." Johnny Zabatino slapped Paulie's back, pulling him into a friendly embrace. "Welcome to the family, Amato. You won't regret this."

They left a minute later, taking their goons with them.

My twin closed his eyes, and I shook him.

"Stef, wake up."

Nothing.

I repeated the same process with Dante.

Nada.

Right before I passed out from the pain rocking through my body, another group of men entered the restaurant.

"What the fuck happened here?" Vincenzo Vitale strolled into the room and stopped in front of the table.

Carlo stood beside him, staring at my father in disbelief. "Who took them out?"

"Johnny Z," I croaked.

Vincenzo and Carlo shoved the table out of the way.

"What did he say?" Joey said to his younger brother, who had given me the scar on my cheek.

The Mafia boss removed his cell phone from his pocket and dialed for help. He told the operator we needed assistance and shoved the phone into his pocket.

"Johnny Z," I repeated.

And then, I lost consciousness.

Chapter Two

NICO

I stared at Paulie, trying to read the lie on his face. He stood in the living room of my penthouse, his white shirt stained with blood. His cheek had a bloody handprint from him raking his fingers over his skin. Paulie often stroked his cheek when he was thinking.

"Dante is on life support," Paulie told us. "He may never wake from a coma."

Ava shook beside me, tears running down her face. "What?" Her hand flew to her mouth, but it didn't help to silence her sobs. "No… How about the twins?"

I curled my arms around her, needing the hug as much as she did. It was so hard to remain calm, pretend like I didn't feel like I was dying on the inside.

"They're in surgery," Paulie explained, his voice tinted with concern that almost felt forced. "Angelo shielded Salvatore and took a few bullets. So did Stefan."

"No, no, no…." Ava's screams pierced my eardrums. "No, they're not allowed to die on me."

My eyes burned from the tears I wanted to spill. But I had to be strong for Ava. She needed me to hold her and say everything would be okay. I couldn't promise that, even though I wanted to believe it.

I cleared my throat. "And my dad?"

Paulie shook his head. "I'm sorry, Nico. Unfortunately, your dad didn't make it."

No.

Turning my head to the side, I swiped at my eyes. I wanted to curl up into a ball and cry. But with Ava clinging to my side, her sobs shaking me, I forced the tears back down.

"I need to see them." Ava tugged on the sleeve of my jacket, pulling my attention back to her. "Take me to the hospital."

"It's not safe," Paulie said before I could respond. "The Vitales picked off your family one by one. If you leave the penthouse, you risk getting whacked." His eyes locked with mine, and then he tipped his head at Ava. "And there's no guarantee for her safety either. This attack was an act of war."

"No," Ava whispered, her voice strained. "We have to see them. I want to be there when Dante wakes up."

"If he wakes up." Paulie's expression turned grim, then slipped into his usual emotionless mask. "The doctor didn't sound optimistic."

"And the twins?"

Paulie rolled his shoulders. "They won't know until after they get out of surgery."

What if they don't make it?

I didn't want to be the boss of the Luciano crime family. It was Dante's right to lead the next generation.

P aulie squeezed my shoulder. "You have to step up as the interim head of the family. The men can't go to war without a leader."

Is he trying to get me whacked?

There were rules in the Mafia. You had to be of one hundred percent Italian descent to be a made man. My dad already broke the old school rules to admit me as a member.

He waited until my twenty-first birthday to tell me the good news. But some of his men rebelled when I became a made man. Some men left to work with other crimes families. Others tried to fight us, only to end up in a shallow grave.

The men who stayed were only here because of their loyalty to my father. They loved and respected

Salvatore Luciano. I doubted they would accept me as the new boss.

But Dante?

Our men would have done anything for him. He was an asshole on his best day, but they would gladly pledge their allegiance to him.

He had to wake up.

"I need to see my dad," I told Paulie, unable to give him an answer.

I'd been suspicious of his unauthorized actives for months. So until I had confirmation my father was dead, my brother's lives in jeopardy, I couldn't trust a fucking word out of his mouth.

Paulie's dark eyebrows rose. "Didn't you hear me, kid? He's dead."

I was almost thirty, and he still called me that. And I fucking hated it. In his eyes, I would always be a kid, the boss's son. A lot of our guys were older, from the previous generation. Dante was only five years older than me, but they didn't see him as a kid.

He'd earned the nickname of *re pazzo*.

Mad king.

I crossed my arms over my suit-clad chest, taking a deep breath through my nose. "I'm not doing anything until I see my family. Dead or alive."

Paulie gave me a light shrug. "Okay, kid. It's your funeral."

He spun on his heels and strolled toward the front door, expecting us to follow him like obedient dogs.

My feet stayed planted on the floor. I couldn't move, let alone think, until I had time to process the situation.

Dad is dead.

Fuck.

"Nico." Ava's voice snapped me out of my head. She clutched my arm and looked up at me, eyes red-rimmed and filled with tears. "You have to take me. I need to see them." Her top lip quivered. "Please."

One look at my beautiful girl, and I got my shit together. For her, I had to be strong.

She needed her rock.

I held out my arm for her to grab hold. "C'mon. Let's go see my brothers."

Chapter Three

AVA

I sat in the waiting room beside Nico, crying on his chest. The tears hadn't stopped flowing since Paulie told us about the shooting. Dante was out of surgery but unconscious. The twins had also pulled through, but we hadn't received any other updates.

They had to live.

Dozens of made men sat in the room with us dressed in black suits. You could tell they weren't businessmen. They had a severe look to their gazes, a hardness to their exteriors.

Nico tapped his fingers on his knee as if he were moving to an imaginary beat. He hadn't spoken much or even cried, trying to stay strong for me. And now, he had men gathered around him, expecting the same.

Nico would be the next boss of the Luciano crime

family if Dante didn't make it. I could see the fear in his eyes when Paulie told him. Even his body language changed.

Salvatore broke the rules when he admitted Nico into the family. But how could he deny his son just because his mother was Irish?

He was still a Luciano.

After an hour of waiting, the mood in the room was somber. All conversation died off, leaving us with background noise from the busy hospital to fill the void. I clung to Nico's side, attempting to steady my rapid heartbeat.

All of Angelo and Stefan's men surrounded us. Nico didn't have a crew of his own, which seemed to create distance between him and the other guys. They didn't speak to Nico the way they did his brothers. He was Paulie's shadow and reported directly to the boss.

Paulie moved in and out of the room, pacing up and down the hallway. Something was off about him. He didn't want us to come to the hospital out of fear we would get whacked. And yet, there wasn't any threat here. Maybe he was overreacting as a precaution, but even Nico thought he was slightly over dramatic.

Several footsteps clicked on the tiled floor as they approached the waiting room. Vincenzo Vitale opened the door with his sons, Joey and Carlo, following. His wife and Vittoria accompanied them, as did the family's advisor.

My eyes widened in shock.

Nico hopped up from the chair, reached beneath his suit, and pointed two guns at them.

The men in the room followed suit, dozens of guns aimed at the Vitales. They were the reason my guys were hanging on for their lives.

"Give me one fucking reason not to kill you," Nico said with a bite to his tone.

"Because we saved your brothers' lives," Vincenzo confessed with a stern but sincere look. "If we hadn't shown up in time to call the ambulance, they would be dead."

Keeping his guns raised, Nico said, "They were meeting you at Monviso. You set the time and place. Not my family."

"We arrived five minutes earlier than scheduled." Vincenzo held up his palms and slowly approached Nico with caution. "Whoever shot your father and brothers left before we got there. I had every intention of brokering peace with Salvatore. Neither of us wanted another war, Nicodemus." He stopped a few feet from Nico. "If I wanted your family dead, they wouldn't be here."

Nico lowered the weapons to his sides.

"Can we speak civilly?" Vincenzo said in a calm tone. "Without shooting each other?"

Nico held his gaze for a long moment before tucking the guns back into the chest holster.

"I'm sorry about your father." Vincenzo put his hand on Nico's shoulder. "He was an honorable man. We were enemies for a long time, but we found common ground over the past few months. I was looking forward to working with him." He paused for a moment. "I hope you will honor our deals in his absence."

"My father's body isn't even cold." Nico's nose scrunched in disgust. "Dante and the twins are still in surgery. We're not speaking about any deals my father made with you."

Vincenzo stuffed his hands into his pockets, and then his gaze drifted to me for a second. "If Dante doesn't survive, will you marry my daughter?"

Nico glanced at me. "Yes."

Disgusted, I shook my head. "You're unbelievable."

Before I could walk away, he wrapped his arms around me. "He's not talking about Vittoria."

I scanned the room, searching for another daughter of Vincenzo Vitale, and only found an angry-looking Vittoria.

"Vincenzo is your real father," Nico said in a hushed tone.

My blood ran ice cold in my veins, the shock of his confession chilling me to the bone.

"No, he's not. Giancarlo Vianello is my dad."

"The night we opened Giancarlo's safe, we found your birth certificate. Someone crossed out Giancarlo's name and wrote Vincenzo's." Nico loosened his grip on me, so I could angle my body to look up at him. "We collected samples from you and Giancarlo and sent them to a lab for DNA testing. You're not Giancarlo's daughter. He couldn't have kids. When we told our dad about the results, he explained that your mom had an affair with Vincenzo."

"She could have had an affair with another man," I pointed out, hoping this was a misunderstanding.

Because that would make Vittoria my half-sister. And after she watched me fuck Nico on the floor and I ended their engagement, I didn't want to face her. How could I ever look at her in the eyes after what we did?

If this were true, I had a sister and two brothers, one of which permanently disfigured one of my boyfriends. Angelo would never forgive Carlo, no matter our relationship.

"It's the truth," Vincenzo said in a hushed tone, keeping the conversation between the three of us. "I was with your mother around the time she conceived you."

It would take more than a peace offering to repair years of discord between our families.

Vincenzo inched toward me, and I couldn't help but wonder if I had any of his features. We both had black hair and brown eyes, nothing special. Thankfully, I had my mother's looks.

My pulse pounded in my ears, making it harder to focus on Vincenzo. Why did my dad pretend all these years? He taught me everything he knew and wanted me to be like him.

Why keep a secret?

He had to have known if he had scratched his name off my birth certificate. At least now, it explained why he stole seven million dollars from my brokerage account and fled the country.

Did he send Mom away for the same reason?

I had many questions, but this wasn't the time or the place. Not with dozens of men listening to our conversation. And especially not with my men still in surgery, not knowing if they would survive.

I had to focus on them.

Anything but the truth.

"I'd like you to come for dinner," Vincenzo said to me, then looked at Nico. "For our families to sit down and discuss the future."

Earlier, he said Nico would have to marry his daughter if Dante didn't make it. The thought rolled around in my head. Was Dante planning to propose to me before he got shot?

We had come a long way, but Dante was still a work in progress. I hadn't even thought about marrying any of the Luciano brothers, least of all Dante. He was the most opposed to a relationship.

"We would love that," I told Vincenzo as if I spoke for the Luciano family. "Once everything settles down."

Vincenzo gave me a closed-mouth smile.

My father.

That word didn't sound normal when speaking about Vincenzo. For most of my life, he was an enemy of the Luciano family. Which also made him my enemy. We wouldn't become besties overnight, but maybe in time, we could find an agreeable resolution to the years of conflict.

Nico extended his hand to Vincenzo. "Thank you for helping my brothers. We'll be in touch."

Vincenzo shook his hand. "If you don't mind, we'd like to stay and see how your brothers make out."

Nico bobbed his head and extended his hand to the right side of the room. There were a handful of vacant chairs. I was surprised that none of the men spoke or expressed their concerns about the Vitales joining us. Some gritted their teeth at Joey and Carlo. But for the most part, it was civilized.

A few more hours passed before a nurse entered the waiting room with the surgeon. "Mr. Luciano?"

Nico stood, bringing me with him. "How are my brothers?"

The doctor stuffed his hands into his pockets, looking slightly nervous. He didn't want to give bad news to a waiting room full of Mafia men.

"Dante hasn't woken up yet. But his vitals look good."

"And the twins?"

"Angelo woke up ten minutes ago. He's still feeling the effects of the drugs, but you can see him if you'd like."

Nico's hands moved to his waist, revealing the guns strapped to his chest. "How about Stefan?"

The nurse and doctor tried to hide their shock and slapped on a straight face. I could recall the first time I met the Luciano brothers. They intimated the fuck out of me. Dante was fourteen years older than me, already a man when I discovered I liked boys. Same with Nico, who was nine years older.

"One of the bullets nearly grazed Stefan's heart," the doctor explained. "He's lucky to be alive."

"Is he awake?" I asked.

The doctor nodded. "Yes, you can see him, too."

"Where are they?"

"Nurse Hannover will take you."

He spoke more about their medical conditions, giving Nico options if they took a turn for the worst. I couldn't bare to listen and tuned him out. After the doctor left the room, the nurse gestured for us to follow her.

"What did he say?" Pete Morelli said to Nico. "Are they gonna make it?"

Nico bobbed his head. "Sounds like it. Angelo and Stefan are out of surgery and awake."

Tony rose from the chair by the window. "How about Dante?"

"They don't know if he'll wake up," Nico explained. "We have to wait and see."

"Fuck." Tony tugged at the ends of his hair. "First, Salvatore. Now, Dante. We can't lose them both."

The guys in the room grunted or nodded in agreement.

They didn't want Nico as their leader.

"We're going to see the twins," Nico told them. "You can go home if you want. I'll call if there's any news about Dante."

"Nah, I'm good." Tony waved him off and sat in the chair beside Pete. "We'll wait it out. I want to see Stefan."

Nico grabbed my hand and led me out of the room. We followed the nurse down a long tiled hallway that stunk of antiseptic. I hated the smell of hospitals.

As we walked, my heart raced with each step, beating so loudly I could hear it in my ears. I reached into my pocket for my inhaler just in case. Keeping it in my sweaty palm, I tried to control my breathing. Nico had enough shit on his plate. He didn't need me collapsing on him.

When we stopped at Dante's room, I halted in the entryway. My mouth hung open at seeing him hooked up to beeping monitors.

Nico tapped my back. "It's okay, *passerotta*. Go ahead."

I took slow, deliberate steps into the room, my pulse pounding as I looked at my sleeping boyfriend.

Could I even call Dante that?

We hadn't defined our relationship.

His eyes were closed, his chest rising and falling. At least he was breathing. I stood at his bedside and leaned down to brush the black hair off his tanned forehead.

"I'm here, Dante. Whenever you're ready, come back to us."

Nico slid his hands to my shoulders.

We didn't need words.

I loved that about him.

He curled his arms around me as I leaned back against his chest. "Do you want to see Angelo and Stefan?"

I nodded.

The twins were in a double occupancy room beside Dante's. Stefan slept soundly with sensors attached to his arms to monitor his vitals, his head turned away from us.

I approached Angelo's bed, which was closer to the door. His eyelids fluttered.

"Angelo," I whispered, placing my hand over his. "Can you hear me?"

One golden-brown eye snapped open, then the other. "Loud and clear, baby."

I ran my fingers down the length of his arm, massaging his skin. "How are you feeling?"

"I've had better days," he quipped, the right corner of his mouth turned up into a smirk. "Nothing I can't handle."

Nico put his hand on my shoulder. "What happened?"

"Dad," Angelo choked out, his voice hoarse. "Did he make it?"

"No." Nico released a deep breath. "He died on site."

"Fuck." Angelo covered his face with his hand, and a sob escaped his throat. He glanced over at Stefan, avoiding our gazes. "How about Dante?"

"He's in a coma," I told him.

Angelo leaned his head back on the thin pillow and

stared at the ceiling, breathing harder. "I'm gonna fucking kill that traitorous prick."

"Who?" Nico stuffed his hands into his pockets, a stern expression on his handsome face. "Dante?"

He shook his head. "Paulie. He fucking sold us out to Johnny Z."

"Wait, what?" I gasped. "Seriously?"

Angelo bobbed his head. "I heard the whole thing before I passed out. Paulie made a deal with Johnny to work for him. And in exchange, he had to turn on us."

"I told Dad we couldn't trust him." Nico bit down on his fist and grunted. "Fucking asshole. He came to my apartment and lied right to my fucking face. Even sat in the waiting room with us and pretended everything was going to be okay."

"He's here?" Angelo's eyes narrowed at his brother. "Are you fucking kidding me?" He threw his hand out at the door. "Get your ass out there and put a bullet in his skull."

"No," I interjected. "Keep your friends close and your enemies closer. Isn't that why you guys forced me to work for you? It will be advantageous if Paulie doesn't know we're on to him."

"I don't like this," Nico said with a hint of anger in his tone. "I agree with Angelo. He needs to go."

I pushed out my hand to silence him. "This isn't what Dante would do."

Nico angled his body to look at me, jaw set hard. "And you think you know my brother so well? Like you know anything about running a crime family?"

He was nervous about possibly becoming the next boss. So I ignored his attitude, but I wasn't dropping the subject.

"I know a lot more about Dante than you think. For the past month, I have shadowed him everywhere. I understand how he thinks. He would keep Paulie around until he figured out if anyone in the family helped him. Then he would get rid of them."

"I don't know," Angelo cut in. "If we let Paulie live, he could feed information to Johnny Z."

"That's exactly why you keep him on as the family advisor. Give him bad information and see if Johnny Z uses it."

"Maybe you should be the boss," Angelo said with laughter in his voice. "You're right. This is what Dante would do." He looked up at Nico, who nodded. "So we'll act like we don't know he helped Johnny Z. Dante will wake up, and when he does, he'll handle Paulie."

Nico expelled a breath of air, relief washing over his face. I didn't blame him for being afraid. He'd just lost his father while his brothers' lives dangled by a thread. The weight of his family's responsibilities sat on his shoulders.

"Dad was right about one thing," Stefan choked

out, snapping my attention to him. "Ava is a fucking genius."

"You're awake." I squealed and ran over to Stefan's bedside. "Oh, my God, Stefan. I was so worried about you." Putting my hand over my heart, I smiled. "Don't do that to me again. I can't lose any of you."

"We're not going anywhere. For better or worse, you're stuck with us." He extended his hand and wiggled his fingers. "Get in here with me, *bellezza*. I got someone who wants to say hello to your sexy ass mouth."

I giggled. "Do you ever stop thinking about sex?"

He shoved the blanket off his legs and pushed up the hospital gown. "Not when you're in the room."

I licked my lips at the sight of him. "How are you hard?" I shook my head in disbelief, a smile gracing my lips. "You just got out of surgery."

"I got shot. I'm not dead." He grabbed my hand and helped me stroke his shaft. "My dick still works."

I leaned over and licked his length, teasing him.

"Fuck, baby, you do that so well," Angelo said when I sucked his twin into my mouth. "When you're done with Stefan, this king could use the royal treatment."

Chapter Four

AVA

After I took care of Angelo and Stefan, I went next door to check on Dante. He was sleeping with the monitors beeping at a steady rate. The nurse assured us his vitals looked good. We just had to wait for him to wake up.

Even if he didn't think anyone liked him—only feared him—that was so far from the truth. All of us loved and respected him. This family didn't work without him issuing orders, leading us the way only Dante knew how.

I sat on his bed and stroked my fingers through his black hair. He looked so handsome, so peaceful. Things had never been easy with Dante. But over the past month, we were growing closer. I was starting to understand why Dante was so close off and didn't let anyone into his life.

I bent down and whispered into his ear, "Please wake up, Dante. We need you." I kissed his cheek. "We love you."

I laid my hand on the bed, and our fingers brushed.

At least his heart was still beating. I hadn't noticed any strange dips in the monitor, staring at it like a hawk.

He was alive.

For now.

I hoped and prayed he would return to us.

I needed him.

We all did.

It sounded strange to me that I would ever say that about Dante. But as I twirled the poker chip and playing card charms on the bracelet he gave me for my birthday, I realized I meant something to him, too. He wouldn't have put this much thought into a present if he didn't care about me.

The day he taught me how to play poker must have stuck with him. It wasn't the greatest of days from the start. But by the night's end, he lowered his guard just enough for me to see what he loved.

Poker.

The casino.

That environment gave him life. It was the one thing that kept him going every day. He enjoyed being the casino boss more than the underboss of the Luciano crime family. At times, I would see the tiniest of smiles gracing his lips. Those stolen moments were few and fleeting, but they were always when we were on the casino floor together.

Dante's finger brushed mine.

I stared at our hands in shock. "Dante, if you can hear me, move your hand again."

"He's not awake," Nico said from the entryway, where he'd been watching me with Dante for the past ten minutes.

Nico had dark circles under his eyes, his usually styled blond hair messy. It looked as if he'd been tugging at the ends. But he was still handsome, his big blue eyes searing my skin.

"Dante moved." I tipped my head at the bed. "Look."

Of course, Dante had to be stubborn and prove me wrong. His hand stayed in the same spot.

Did I imagine him touching me?

I hadn't slept in over twenty-four hours and was running on fumes. My mind could have been playing tricks on me. But when I felt his skin touch mine once more, a smile stretched the corners of my mouth.

I looked at Nico. "Did you see that?"

He bobbed his head, a tiny smile on his face. Nico didn't attempt to move any farther into the room. Instead, he let me have this moment with Dante. One of the many things I loved about Nico was that he knew when to let me be.

Nico's phone rang, cutting through the silence. He spoke to someone in Italian, his voice low and controlled, and after a minute, he pocketed the phone.

"I have to help Paulie with something," he said. "But I shouldn't be long. If you need anything, Tony, Vinnie, and Pete are in the waiting room."

"I'm fine right here."

He held my gaze for a moment as if trying to capture one more second before disappearing into the hallway. The twins had fallen asleep after the nurse gave them more medicine. And since Dante was finally showing real signs of life, I was staying put.

I couldn't believe Paulie betrayed the family after thirty years as Salvatore's advisor. It had to be about more than money. The Don paid him well and treated him like family. When Dante woke up, he would get the truth out of Paulie, one way or another.

I curled up beside Dante and watched his chest rise and fall, running my fingers through his hair. He hated any form of human affection. So I had to take in every inch of him while I could. He would wake up, and when he did, we would return to our no-touching rules.

At least an hour passed without Nico returning to the room. Dante moved again, and this time, his eyelids fluttered.

"Dante?" I brushed my fingers across his jaw. "Dante, can you hear me?"

Chapter Five

DANTE

White light blinded me when I opened my eyes. I blinked a few times, my eyelids heavy. Fuck, my head hurt, pounding like a drum from the stabbing pain at the base of my skull. My tongue stuck to the roof of my mouth, and I couldn't even produce enough spit to swallow.

I focused on the light overhead, which seemed to get brighter the longer I stared.

Am I dead?

In Heaven?

God wouldn't let me into Heaven with all of the horrible shit I had done. So if this was Hell, the Devil was playing tricks on me, fucking with my head.

Clearing the sleep from my eyes, I tried to adjust to my surroundings. The small room had a shitty fabric chair in the corner. Ava's Bottega Veneta purse, a birthday gift from Stefan, hung over the arm.

Most of the room was sparse. Monitors beeped, connected to the sensor on my arm. I could see a bathroom through the crack in a partially open door.

I'm in a hospital.

All at once, the memories from Monviso came flooding back to me.

The shooting.

My father dying.

Paulie's betrayal.

Nico was right about not trusting Paulie. Our dad was too out of his mind to see it. He hadn't been himself for a while, always forgetting shit. It was Paulie's job to speak on behalf of our father, especially when negotiating with other crime families. But he had gotten too involved, venturing out on his own.

We all saw it.

But not Dad.

He was too trusting of his friends.

Look what it got him.

I tried to sit up and felt something tear on my right side.

Fuck.

Excruciating pain shot down my body, setting my skin on fire. I wasn't sitting in this bed or staying another second in a hospital. So I gripped the bed's side rail and breathed through my nose, attempting to get up again. I had to get out of this fucking place and find my brothers.

If they were alive…

The last I remembered, Angelo and Stefan used the table to shield us from the onslaught of bullets. Dad took several to the chest and passed out beside me. I would never forget the moment his eyes closed.

I knew.

He was dead.

The past was repeating itself. I was by my mother's side when she took one last look at me, the life draining from her body. And now, my dad was gone, which meant our family needed a new leader. I'd prepared for this my entire life. But I thought I would be much older when my father stepped down.

The door creaked open, letting in the noise from the bustling hallway. A staff of doctors and nurses flew past my room, pushing a gurney.

"You're alive." Ava sat on the bed beside me and expelled a breath of air, relief washing over her face. "Let me get the nurse."

As she attempted to slide off the bed, I grabbed her arm. "No."

"But the doctor needs to check on you," Ava insisted with a tinge of panic in her tone. "You almost died. Just give me a second." She patted my hand. "I'll come right back."

"Ava," I whispered, eyes barely open but focused on her. "Water."

"Yeah, okay."

She rushed into the adjoined bathroom, filled a small plastic cup with water from the faucet, and tilted the cup to my lips.

I drank small sips until I finished the water.

"Do you want more?"

I shook my head. "Where are my brothers?"

"Nico is with Paulie."

My eyes widened at her confession.

"Get him on the phone." My jaw hurt from clenching. "Now. He's not safe with Paulie." My voice was deeper than usual and scratchy. "That piece of shit sold us out."

"Nico knows," she said, tapping her fingers nervously on the bed. "Since you were out of commission, we all agreed to pretend we didn't know Paulie was involved. So that we could keep him close to the family to feed him bad information." When I didn't speak or acknowledge her comment, she added, "It was my suggestion. I thought that was what you would do."

A proud smile graced my lips. "Good girl. You've been paying attention."

We'd spent a lot of time together over the past few months. Ava could run the casino in my absence. She was a fast learner and had proven we could trust her.

"Nico knows what to do," Ava said with confidence. "He'll be okay with Paulie."

As if saying his name summoned him, Nico appeared in the entryway. He stood there with his hands on his hips, suit jacket pushed to the side to reveal two weapons.

I gripped the side rail, my hand trembling from exerting too much energy. "Where are the twins?"

"They're fine," Ava cut in. "Next door. Last time I checked, they were sleeping off the pain meds."

Nico put his hand over his heart as he entered the room. "Fuck, Dante. I didn't think you were ever going to wake up."

I bet he was scared. Nico would have become the next leader of the Boardwalk Mafia if I died. We lost men over our father making Nico part of the family. They didn't see him as a legitimate heir.

Not like me.

I was Sicilian on both sides of the family. My uncle ruled Calabria, while my father held his position in Atlantic City for over thirty years.

Now, it was my turn.

"Thanks for the vote of confidence," I shot back at Nico with my usual attitude.

Nico wasn't my favorite. But he was beginning to grow on me. It only took thirty years to see he wasn't completely useless. He had Ava to thank for that.

Stefan and Angelo staggered into the room a few minutes later. They must have overheard our conversation from their beds.

Thank God they were okay.

I cared for the twins as if they were my children and couldn't bear the thought of losing them, too.

"Daddy's awake," Angelo joked, moving past Nico to stand at my bedside.

He started that shit after Ava arrived to annoy me. They both gained pleasure from torturing me with their childish humor.

"Don't call me that," I hissed.

"All better, I see." Angelo laughed. "Almost dying didn't change your attitude one bit."

Ignoring his stupid comment, I tried to get out of bed, but it hurt like fucking hell. I groaned, clutching my right side.

Nico pushed out his hand to stop me. "Let me help you."

I gave him a warning look to stay the fuck away from me. "I can do it myself."

He held up his hands in surrender. "I'm only trying to be nice. It wouldn't kill you to accept help from us."

"I'm fine," I tossed back with even more anger in my tone.

"No, you're not." Ava sighed. "I'm getting the doctor. Don't move."

"I'll go," Nico offered and disappeared into the hallway.

I pointed at the chairs across the room. "The two of you sit. We have a lot to discuss."

"You haven't been awake ten minutes," Ava protested. "Rest and get better before you start plotting revenge."

Maybe she hadn't learned enough from me. Avenging my father's death was all I could think about. By some miracle, the three of us survived. And I wasn't going to waste my second chance at life.

I gripped her chin until her eyes met mine, even though it was painful to raise my arm. "I'm the boss of this family now. And you listen to me."

A cute smile touched her lips, a defiant look in her pretty brown eyes. "Yes, Daddy."

I shook my head, letting my hand drop to the bed. "One day, I'm going to kill you for calling me that."

"No, you're not." She kissed my cheek. "I think you secretly love it."

Chapter Six

AVA

Five days had passed since Dante woke up. He tried to get out of bed and leave the hospital dozens of times. Dante even threatened the doctor, who insisted he stay for more observation. But after I convinced him to stay until the end of the week, he stopped fighting everyone.

Dante passed out from the pain meds an hour ago. So I curled up beside him and tried to take a nap. It was hard with all of the people walking by the room. The loud voices over the intercom in the hallway didn't help. But Dante was dead to the world, his chest rising and falling in the perfect rhythm.

He was alive.

The twins were with the physical therapist. Nico was at Salvatore's apartment with Paulie, planning the funeral. They went over the entire estate, including Salvatore's death plan. He was a very meticulous man and wanted everything a certain way.

His funeral would be a televised event. Not by his choice but because he was a local celebrity. People loved Salvatore and were coming from around the world to say goodbye.

After an hour of trying to sleep, I slid off the bed and stretched my arms above my head, yawning. Turning to look at Dante, I said, "I'm going to the cafeteria for coffee. I'll be right back."

He didn't move an inch.

I took the elevator to the ground floor and followed the signs to the cafeteria. With Dante and the twins stuck at the hospital, I lived here. Nico brought my clothes from home. The staff even rolled a bed into Dante's room so I could sleep beside him.

He was an important man in this town. The same rules other guests had to follow didn't apply to us. We didn't have regular visiting hours, though Dante refused to see anyone other than his brothers.

A few times, he spoke to Paulie but wouldn't look him in the eye. He was good at pretending not to hate him. For a long time, he even had me fooled. But now, we were inseparable.

Dante didn't make me leave. He seemed to like having me by his side. We ate meals together. I read books to him from the Kindle app on my phone. At night, we watched TV together. I wasn't all that surprised that he liked to watch Jeopardy and knew most of the answers. In the past week, I learned a lot more about Dante. But I could tell it was killing him to stay in this bed and listen to the doctor's orders.

Whenever he tried to leave, I talked him into staying. Once, he even called me Boss. His Don. It was so fucking cute that I couldn't stop smiling.

I poured myself a cup of hot chocolate and took a few sips, thinking about the cup I drank last night while I watched TV with Dante. He kissed me and said I tasted delicious, and he couldn't get enough of me.

On my way down the hallway, headed back upstairs, a man dressed in a suit approached me. He was in his forties and had dark brown hair. "Miss Vianello, you need to come with me."

Vinnie Corallo worked for Stefan and hung out at Lucky's a lot. We'd met over the past few months, but I hadn't spoken much to him. He always gave Stefan a hard time and mocked him. However, Stefan didn't seem to mind.

I stopped in front of him. "What's wrong?"

He extended his hand to me. "Dante sent me. He says you're not safe in the hospital and need to come with me back to the Portofino."

I bit my lip, confused about why Dante would send someone for me.

Why didn't Nico come?

Or even Tony?

I didn't know Vinnie as well as Tony, but he was one of Stefan's most trusted men. So I placed my free hand in his and let him lead the way. Vinnie ushered me through the bustling hospital, dodging orderlies pushing wheelchairs and anxious-looking patients.

When we reached the elevator bank, he yanked on my arm and steered me in the opposite direction.

"Hey, what are you doing?" I slapped his arm to get him off me, but he didn't release his grip. "Why are you taking me this way?"

"Shortcut," he said, his voice devoid of emotion.

Vinnie pushed open a back door marked *Fire Exit.* Outside, he guided me over to a black SUV with tinted windows. The front window was down so that I could see a man in the passenger seat. It wasn't Tony or any guys I'd seen around the casino.

My stomach knotted as we moved toward the vehicle. It was too dark to make out the man's features.

I threw my weight into Vinnie's side, attempting to knock him off balance. "I want to go upstairs. Let me go."

Another man got out of the SUV and grabbed my

arm, squeezing hard. My foot made contact with his body as he dragged me toward the open door.

"Get off me!"

I tried to elbow him in the stomach and missed. His hand covered my mouth, and the scent of tobacco on his skin was enough to knock me out.

"She's being difficult," he said to a man in the car, who opened the door and got out.

He walked toward us and reached into his pocket. But I couldn't make out his features in the darkness.

I only smelled him.

Heard him breathe.

And then, he jammed a needle into my neck, taking away my will to fight.

Chapter Seven

AVA

I woke up on the dirty floor of an oversized office. A migraine drilled into my skull, making it hard to keep my eyes open. Thankfully, the room was dark, lit by a lamp, which cast a soft glow.

I scanned the room, my heart thundering in my chest. The desk in front of me had phonebooks stacked almost to the ceiling. There were metal shelves to my right, overflowing with boxes of women's heels and lingerie. Various pieces of junk littered most of the room.

I heard noises on the other side of the door.

People shouting.

Loud music.

A bass beat somewhere in the distance, thumping

through the walls and sending vibrations down my back and legs.

I pushed my palm to the wall and tried to stand, but I was still groggy from the drugs and off balance. My shoulder crashed into the wall. I sank back to the floor with a groan.

Fuck.

Bile pricked the back of my throat, rising from my stomach. The room spun when I tried to focus on anything for too long. So I closed my eyes and tried to regain my bearings.

I had faith in Nico. He would return to Dante's hospital room and realize someone had taken me. I wondered how many of their men had turned on them.

Could they trust anyone?

Fear slid down my spine like spiders crawling over my skin. If Vinnie was helping Paulie, then my men could be in danger at the hospital.

I started to doze off when the door creaked open. A soft yellow light filtered into the dark room.

Vinnie stepped inside with a wicked grin on his lips. He tugged at the cufflink on his left sleeve and stalked toward me.

"Where am I?" I slid my back along the wall to get away from him. "Why are you doing this?"

He shook his head, amused. A deep cackle escaped his lips as he lifted a black thong and bra from a shelf and tossed it onto the tiled floor in front of me. "Change into this. It's almost showtime."

"I'm not wearing that. Or taking off my clothes for you."

"Not like it matters." He laughed. "You'll be taking your clothes off in front of a much larger audience."

"Like fucking hell I am." I used every ounce of my strength to push myself up from the floor. "Where are we?"

"A strip club," he said with a bored expression. "The best in the city."

We weren't at Lucky's. So that left one of Johnny Zabatino's clubs. He owned more strip clubs and bars than the other crime families. Most of the places were local watering holes full of criminals and drunks. They weren't upscale like the businesses owned by the Lucianos.

I peeked up at the man towering over me. "Do you expect me to dance for you?"

Vinnie licked his lips and nodded. "You can start with me. Let me get a good look at the pussy that has the Luciano brothers so whipped."

I balled my hands into fists at my sides. "You're disgusting."

"And you're a dirty whore about to get auctioned off to the highest bidder." He bent down and lifted the bra and thong from the floor, dangling them on his index finger. "Get dressed. I won't tell you again."

I crossed my arms under my breasts and rolled my eyes. "Go fuck yourself!"

"Take off your clothes. Now!"

I shook my head. "You're a real piece of shit. Stefan trusted you, treated you like family. And you turn your back on him."

"Don't act like you understand me or my reasons," he fired back with venom in his tone, nostrils flaring. "You have three seconds to take off your clothes and get fucking ready." He flung the lingerie at me and produced a knife from the inner pocket of his suit jacket, a long one with a beveled handle. "Before I cut the fabric off your body."

He said the last part with a sly grin. Vinnie "The Knife" Corallo didn't get that name because he liked to play with knives. If the rumors in Atlantic City were true, he gutted his enemies like a fish and sent scraps of their skin to their families. Sick and twisted, he was probably even worse than Dante.

I picked up the underwear from the floor and sighed.

What choice do I have?

I wanted to run, but my better judgment told me to do as he instructed. So I pulled the shirt over my head and dropped it onto the grimy tile. My jeans and sneakers were the next addition to the pile.

"Why can't I wear my bra and panties?"

A cocky smirk tipped up the right side of his mouth. "You wear what the boss wants."

My pain was his pleasure.

I could see it in his eyes.

Read it on his face.

He watched as I unhooked my bra and slid the straps down my shoulders. I quickly put on the black lace bra. Sucking in a deep breath, I mentally prepared myself for the last part as I pushed my panties over my hips and put on the thong.

Vinnie didn't take his eyes off my body, standing inches away with his hands shoved into his black slacks.

"Why are you working for Johnny Z?" I shook my head, still in disbelief about the situation. "That's a downgrade from the Lucianos. And you know it."

Jaw clenched, he gripped my arm, digging his fingers into my bicep. "You never know when to shut your mouth."

Pain radiated up the left side of my body as he dragged me down a long, dimly lit hallway painted a deep shade of red that almost looked black. Music floated through the air. Without breaking stride, Vinnie opened a steel door and pushed through it.

We were backstage, a curtain separating us from the main entertainment at the club. My heart thumped in my ears, growing louder than the music belting from the speakers. Men cheered and shouted on the other side.

"It's time to make your debut, little whore."

Vinnie peeled back the curtain with one hand and moved me onto the stage. A raging crowd of men spread throughout the club at tables. Poles bolted into the ceiling, mirrored walls reflected every inch of skin on display in the large, open room.

Cigar and cigarette smoke clung to the air, thick like fog. The lights were too bright, forcing me to shield my eyes with my forearm. Perfume and cologne permeated the air. It was a horrible smell, one that made my lungs work harder.

Blinking a few times, I tried to clear my vision. And when my eyes adjusted to the brightness, my mouth widened in shock. Johnny Z sat at a table in front of the stage with two men beside him.

He was maybe a few years older than Dante and had dark brown hair that flopped onto his forehead. Like all made men, he wore a suit and a blood-red silk tie.

When our eyes met, he leaned forward, his palms

on the wooden table, grinning. "Do you know who I am?"

I nodded.

He looked at the man beside him. "What do you think, Carmine? Is she hot enough to get the Luciano brothers to come running over here?"

"If Dante Luciano thinks her pussy is special, it's got to be worth something." Carmine scrubbed a hand across his jaw, eyes on Johnny, and laughed. "I wonder if she tastes as good as she looks."

"Only one way to find out," Johnny said with a cocky smirk. "Time we repaid the Lucianos for fucking with our family, don't you think?"

With a simple nod, Carmine communicated with Johnny and hopped onto the stage with me. I stepped backward toward the curtain, and Vinnie grabbed my ass.

Sandwiched between two men, I had at least a hundred pairs of eyes on my almost naked body. More men than I could count were in the audience, cheering and shouting dirty comments at me.

"Let's go, honey," a man yelled. "Shake that ass for us."

Johnny raised his hand to silence him. He locked onto me and licked his lips. "Take something off, *puttana.* You're wearing too much clothing for my liking." He dragged his teeth across his lip. "I need to see what I'm getting in return."

"Take off your bra," Vinnie ordered as he slid his finger beneath the strap. "You don't want to disappoint us."

I shook my head, covering my breasts with my hands.

Vinnie tugged on the right strap while Carmine pulled down the other. It was no use. If I didn't cooperate, they would only make this worse for me. One way or another, the clothes were coming off.

Men raised numbered cards on sticks.

Money changed hands.

They placed bids on me.

When I didn't move fast enough, Carmine removed a gun from his back pocket and held the cold metal to my forehead. "Let's go. We don't have all night, princess."

Biting my bottom lip, I unhooked the bra straps, biting back the tears. It was degrading and horrifying, and I was scared for my life. I held the material over my nipples, which only pissed off the audience even more.

Men screamed obscenities.

Some yelled at me.

My ears rang from so much noise, and I could hardly focus on them. The room spun around me, the drugs still wearing on me. I wasn't sure how much time had passed from when they drugged me until now, but I still didn't have good balance. So when I lost my footing, Vinnie hooked his arm around me.

Johnny kept his eyes on me. "Take it off. Now!"

He was losing his patience with me. With tears sliding down my cheeks, I let the fabric fall to the floor at my feet, baring myself to this monster and the pigs in the room. Men whistled and howled, shouting for me to keep going.

Johnny tapped his fingers on his thigh. "Dance for us."

A song blared through the overhead speakers, piercing my eardrums. I was too tired, hungry, and scared to process the song's name. It sounded familiar, a rock beat I'd heard before, but I couldn't place it.

I moved my hips back and forth, holding back the tears that welled in my bottom lids.

Johnny snapped his fingers. "Look at me. Smile for the camera."

"The Luciano brothers will give you whatever you want," I said, hoping to persuade him. "Just let me make a call."

He gave me a shit-eating grin. "If the Luciano brothers want you back, they have to bid like everyone else."

I sucked in a deep breath, telling myself I could do this. It was just skin.

Carmine took photos and video and handed the phone to Johnny for approval.

He skimmed through the footage and nodded. "Let's see how much trouble she's worth."

When I stepped off the elevator with Paulie, half the men in the waiting room had cleared out. Pete and Tony propped up against each other, sleeping. Three guys who worked for Angelo were on the opposite side of the room, eating sandwiches from the wrappers.

"Hey, kid." Paulie tapped my arm. "I'm going to run down to the cafeteria. You want anything?"

I looked at the cheesesteak in Mike's hand, my stomach rumbling from the delicious scent of steak and onions. "Yeah, get me one of those steaks."

Paulie slapped me on the back to acknowledge my request. He got back into the elevator. I headed in the opposite direction, past the waiting room and the nurse's station.

I poked my head into Dante's room, surprised to find Ava missing. She was at my brother's side a few hours ago.

If Ava wasn't with Dante, she had to be with the twins. So I entered their room, but Ava wasn't there.

What the fuck?

I checked the entire floor, stopping to ask the nurses and doctors if they had seen her. She was beautiful and hard to miss. By the time I inspected every room, including the bathrooms, I was breathless.

I returned to the twins' room.

They were awake and watching TV, laughing at a movie on the screen. The doctor expected a smooth recovery. Dante was lucky to be alive.

"Have you guys seen Ava?" I placed my palms on my knees to catch my breath. "I ran up and down this fucking place. Can't find her."

Angelo sat up straight and groaned, clutching his side as if he'd ripped his stitches. "Fuck," he bit out. "When was the last time you saw her?"

"I left her in Dante's room. But that was a few hours ago." I moved between their beds. "She wouldn't leave the hospital without telling one of us."

"Maybe she went to the cafeteria," Stefan suggested.

"I checked there."

Which reminded me…

Paulie never came back with my food, and I didn't see him down there. That fucking cock sucking pig. I should have put a bullet in Paulie's head after Angelo told us about his betrayal.

"The hospital has cameras." Angelo slung his legs over the side of the bed and put his bare feet on the cold tile. "Call Dante's hacker." He snapped his fingers. "What's his name?"

"Slade."

"Yeah." Angelo bobbed his head. "Call him. Get him to hack into the cameras and find Ava."

Slade Rizzoli did a lot of shady work for our family. Dante saved his ass from going to jail. Now he owed us and helped Dante do lot of illegal shit.

I removed my cell phone from my pocket and dialed Slade. He answered on the second ring, and I explained the situation. It didn't take more than a few minutes before he sent me a link to the live camera feed.

I hung up and went back to the moment I left Ava. She lay on the bed with Dante, curled up on her side. Our girl looked so peaceful, touching my brother in his sleep because it was the only time she would get away with it. I wanted to laugh but wasn't in the mood. Not without knowing where she went.

I stopped at the point when she left Dante's room. Angelo was out of bed, leaning into my shoulder, his eyes on the screen. It would take more than a bullet to keep Angelo in that bed.

When I finally found Ava, an ache tore through my stomach like a knife to the gut, driving in so deep I could hardly fucking stand up straight.

"Vinnie Corallo," Angelo said with anger in his tone. "You gotta be fucking kidding me."

Of all the men to kidnap our girl, I never would have expected Vinnie to go against the family. He was a loyal soldier and had been for years. We watched the rest of the video as Vinnie led Ava outside through a fire exit.

Johnny Zabatino got out of a black SUV and stabbed Ava with a needle. He tossed the syringe on the ground, and when Ava swayed into his arm, he threw her at Carmine Figarello.

Johnny's second-in-command.

Carmine lifted Ava into the back seat of the SUV and got in beside her. Johnny hopped into the passenger and let his newest recruit drive. I couldn't believe Vinnie turned on us.

"Stef, you need to see this." Angelo threw my phone onto his bed.

He watched in awe, and his mouth hung open in surprise. "What the fuck?" His eyes lifted to meet mine. "Is this real?"

I nodded. "Vinnie took Ava."

"That fucking *pompinaro*." Teeth gritted teeth, he wrapped his fingers around the phone. "I trusted him."

A text message dinged on my phone. Stefan held it out for me to see the message from an unknown number. I tapped the screen to open the video, and my blood ran cold when I hit Play.

It was Ava.

She was on a stage, hiding her face with her hair as they forced her to strip for a crowd of men screaming and waving paddles with numbers in their hands.

They were bidding on her.

Fuck.

I bit down on my fist, anger coursing through my veins. "This is my fault. I shouldn't have left her alone."

Angelo clutched my shoulder. "I will kill every last one of them."

Stefan breathed through his nose, shaking his head. "Calm down, Lo. At least we know where they're keeping her. The stupid fucks didn't think to film away from the mirrored wall."

I lifted an eyebrow at him. "You know where she's at?"

"That looks like The Red Room." Stefan held out his hand. "Let me get another look."

If anyone knew the interior of any strip club in the city, it was my brother. Stefan prided himself on knowing all of our competition and eliminating them.

Stefan replayed the video when Angelo sat on the bed beside him. "Recognize this place?"

"Definitely The Red Room," Angelo confirmed with a nod.

Angelo shot up from the bed way too fast for his injuries. Blood seeped through the hospital gown, right over his shoulder, but he didn't seem to give a fuck. If he was in pain, I couldn't tell. My younger brother wasn't in the right frame of mind.

None of us were.

Even though I knew they should stay and get some rest, I needed their help. They were the only people in this town I trusted.

We had to find Ava.

The clock at the bottom of the screen indicated we had less than twenty-four hours to either bid and win or find her.

"Drive us to The Red Room," Angelo said with his back to me as he stripped off the gown. He walked around the room naked until he found his blood-stained clothes.

Stefan dressed into his suit and tapped me on the shoulder. "Let's go, Pretty Boy. The clock is ticking."

Before we left the hospital, I stopped in the waiting room and woke up Pete and Tony. I told them about

Vinnie's betrayal, and they were just as surprised that Vinnie turned on us.

I ordered them to watch Dante's room. They spent a lot of time with Vinnie, but I didn't suspect either of them of foul play.

Neither did Stefan.

I rode the elevator with Stefan and Angelo down to the ground floor and drove us to The Red Room. Cars packed the parking lot. A dozen of our men met us there, splitting into teams to secure the perimeter of the building.

"Follow my lead," Angelo said and then took off toward the back of the club.

We rounded the side of the building. Stefan moved in front of us, pulled open the back door, and disappeared inside.

Where was the security?

All strip clubs had guards to deal with drunk, rowdy men. Some people got stupid when they had too much to drink and tried to shoot up the place. Even at a high-end gentleman's club like Lucky's, Stefan still had issues with regulars.

Gun in hand, and Angelo covering my back, I took one step into the club. But Angelo tugged on my shoulder, right as a bullet sunk into the metal door.

One more.

Then another.

"We can't leave Stefan," Angelo whispered. "Go around the building. There's another entrance the girls use. It leads to the dressing rooms."

While it was my job to follow Paulie and learn how to be my father's *consigliere*, my brothers preferred to stick with gambling and whores. They knew their way around a club.

Angelo glanced up at the security camera on the wall. He waited until it turned to the left before he got in front of me and inched along the wall. I followed behind him, glancing over my shoulder.

We walked through a large dressing room full of vanities and racks of clothes and then headed down the hallway. Angelo peeled back a curtain and took a few steps back, his gun drawn and ready to fire.

A few seconds later, Stefan ran through the curtain past us. "Let's go!"

We took off down the hall with two men trailing behind us. They fired several shots, which barely missed my ear. Angelo and Stefan ran out the door. They waited off to the side of a dumpster at the edge of the parking lot while I ducked beside a sports car for cover. The two men followed me, continuing to shoot.

I made it back to my car as another shot hit the fender. The three of us got into the car, and Stefan peeled out of the lot.

I gripped the back of his seat and realized he was bleeding. "You need a doctor."

"I'm fine," Stefan assured me. "Nothing a bottle of whiskey and a blow job can't fix."

I shook my head. "Suit yourself."

Angelo glanced out the window. "They filmed the video at the club but weren't holding the auction there."

"We didn't get a good enough look to know for sure," I pointed out.

Stefan rolled down the window and hung his arm out the side. "Angelo is right. They lured us here to finish the job. Ava wasn't at the club for long. I poked my head onto the stage before they caught me. They had four bachelor parties and a bunch of college kids. Not the kind of clientele who bid of women."

"We have to find her," I said with anger in my tone, not meant for my brothers.

"I'll search every club he owns, break down every fucking door in this city," Stefan bit out. "We'll find our girl. And then we'll kill that slimy piece of shit and everyone who helped him."

Chapter Nine

AVA

I woke up with a migraine from the drugs Johnny's men put in my water. One minute, I was on stage and stripping for a bunch of degenerates. The next, they brought me into the back room at the club and drugged me.

They said the auction would end tomorrow. That gave the Luciano brothers less than twenty hours to find me. Although, I was losing track of time, unsure of where Johnny was keeping me.

I scanned the unfamiliar room.

White walls.

Bars on the windows.

Only a bed.

I pushed myself up from the mattress and let my

legs dangle off the edge. A sliver of natural light filtered in through the white curtains. But you couldn't miss the cage-like effect the bars on the windows provided.

This was worse than hell.

A literal prison.

I once thought my men caged me like a bird. Now, I could see how much freedom they allowed me, even when I was their captive.

Their pawn.

I wanted to kill Johnny Zabatino. Rip his eyeballs from his skull and shove them down his throat. That asshole humiliated me.

But I had no choice.

Strip or die.

At least now, I was wearing a T-shirt. A white V-neck with no bra and a pair of lace panties. A vast improvement from the last time I was conscious.

I shot up from the bed, ready to fight, and raised my fists when the door creaked open. It was a woman with long reddish brown hair and big blue eyes. She was pretty, her skin free of makeup.

The girl stopped in the entryway and laughed, shaking her head. "We got ourselves a fighter. Don't waste your time, sweetie. Bravery will not get you far in this house."

"Who are you?" I inched toward her, keeping my hands out in front of me. "Where am I?"

She waved her hand to dismiss me. "I can't help you. But don't worry. This won't last long. You'll be with your new master soon."

Master?

Fuck, no.

"I'm Raven." She moved her hands to her narrow hips. "And it's your turn to wake Johnny."

"What?"

I cringed at the thought.

"You're one of Johnny's girls until the auction ends." She clutched my wrists and urged me to lower my arms at my sides. "Better get dressed. Johnny doesn't like cold food."

Waves of nausea washed over me, the bile rising from my stomach choking me.

Raven entered the closet, and when she emerged, she handed me skimpy black lingerie. "Put this on."

After I dressed, Raven guided me into the hallway lined with armed guards. A dark-haired man wearing a black suit gave me a tray of food. Raven placed her hand on my back and guided me down the corridor.

Johnny's bedroom had a sitting area, oversized bathroom, and a four-poster bed built for a king.

"Perfect timing." Johnny smoothed a hand through

his dark, wavy hair and sat up in bed. He patted the mattress. "Get over here."

I stepped into the room, the tray shaking from my trembling hands. The doors closed behind me, leaving me alone in the lion's den.

Johnny rolled onto his side, a pair of tight gray boxer briefs hugging his muscular thighs. He propped his elbow on a pillow and looked at me. "Feed me."

I put the tray on the bed and picked up the fork and knife. With some hesitation, I cut the omelet. But Johnny gripped my wrist, his long fingers warm and surprisingly soft.

He rubbed my skin, right over the vein, with his thumb. "Start with the fruit."

I poked a slice of pineapple with the fork, and Johnny pushed out his hand to stop me. "With your fingers."

Disgusted, I pinched a pineapple cube between my fingers and held it in front of Johnny's mouth. He sank his teeth into the fruit, the juice dripping down my hand. Then he took my finger and sucked it into his mouth.

My eyes went wide with shock. I attempted to remove my finger, but Johnny gripped my wrist tight and held my hand in place. He licked every bit of the juice from my skin before releasing his hold on me.

"You taste good," he growled in a deep tone that sent a shiver down my arms. "I can't wait to taste the rest of you."

I swallowed the lump at the back of my throat. "Your eggs are getting cold."

He smirked. "I'd rather eat you."

I stabbed at the omelet with the fork.

Johnny cupped his hand over mine, forcing me to look at him. "You're a beautiful girl, Ava." His voice was so smooth and sensual. "I still haven't decided what to do with you."

"Let me go," I begged, hating how pathetic and small my voice sounded.

"I can't do that."

"The Luciano brothers will pay whatever you want."

Johnny hesitated for a second before he said, "You belong to me."

"Do you know who I am?"

He shrugged. "Does it matter?"

"Yes, it does. You will start a war if you keep me here. My father is Vincenzo Vitale."

Johnny released his grip on me and slid his hands behind his head. "War is good for business. It helps us make room for a new regime. That's how I became the boss."

"The Luciano brothers will kill you for this," I said through gritted teeth.

Johnny hit a button on a black box next to him. "Send Raven in here."

A minute later, the doors opened. Raven pranced into Johnny's bedroom in a white lacy bra and matching thong. She smiled at him as if he was her entire world.

Raven came up to Johnny's side of the bed and waited for him to slide his hand up her thigh, stopping at the thin string of her underwear. "Everything okay, Boss?"

He ripped the delicate fabric from her body, a crooked smile curling up the corners of his mouth.

This was getting too weird.

Johnny played with Raven, stealing moans from her parted lips, staring at me while he fingered her. His cock tented his boxer briefs, his length growing with each moan. As much as I wanted to look away, I understood this was part of the game.

So I didn't lower my gaze.

After he made Raven come with his fingers, Johnny pushed his boxers over his hips and threw them at me. Johnny leaned back against the headboard and pulled Raven on top of him. He gripped her hips, with his eyes fixed on me, and bounced her up and down, making a hissing sound as he thrust deeper inside her.

She moaned.

He growled.

Raven closed her eyes.

Johnny winked at me.

Sick fuck.

They forced me to watch the show for at least a half hour. Johnny bent her over the bed for the finale, looking at me as he pulled out and came on her back. It was as if he was writing his damn name on her.

Johnny slapped Raven's ass and ordered her to get in the shower. She staggered toward the bathroom door like she was so thoroughly fucked she couldn't remember her name. Dante left me feeling the same way after our first time.

With his dick glistening with cum, Johnny walked to the right side of the bed and hit the button on his nightstand. His doorman appeared a second later, gesturing for me to follow.

Johnny pointed his long finger at me. "Get rid of her. We're going through with the original plan." Johnny wiped his cock with a tissue from his bedside table. "She's not going to work out."

The man dragged me out of the room, the door slamming behind us, and escorted me down the hall. He stopped in front of my bedroom, unlocked the door, and threw me inside like a garbage sack. I fell to the floor, scraping my knees.

Hugging my legs to my chest, I glanced up at him with tears in my bottom lids.

He wasn't worth my tears.

Neither was Johnny.

We exchanged a brief second of silence before he locked me inside my prison.

Chapter Ten

NICO

I shoved Carmine Figarello onto the plank in the warehouse's basement with a gun to his head. Angelo strapped down his legs, and Stefan fastened his wrists above his head to the wooden board.

Carmine was Johnny Z's second in command and from the old regime. Nothing and no one could scare him. I had to look hard, but the fear was evident in his eyes. He hadn't spoken since we dragged his sorry ass out of a whorehouse with his pants down, mid-blowjob.

I reached for the jug of water on the table and handed it to Angelo. Like Dante, he reveled in the fear of others. His eyes lit with excitement as he popped the top from the bottle.

He got off on their screams.

Enjoyed their pain.

Stefan held a dirty rag over Carmine's mouth and nose while Angelo tipped the water bottle. His body thrashed from the excruciating torture of feeling like he was drowning, begging to break free from his shackles. Even the toughest men couldn't handle waterboarding. It was one of the cruelest forms of torture.

"Where's Johnny hiding Ava?" I yelled at Carmine.

When I was younger, Dante showed me waterboarding techniques. It was one of the few times we got along. Lately, Ava was bringing us together. My brothers never treated me the same, but now that we were sharing one woman, it was bonding us in ways I had dreamed of when we were kids.

Angelo eased up for a second, lifting the rag to give him a chance to answer. Carmine turned his head to the side and coughed on the water.

"Answer me," I demanded.

"You're gonna kill me no matter what," Carmine muttered, out of breath, gasping for air. "Go ahead and fucking do it."

Angelo repeated the same process as before. This asshole would tell us what we wanted, or he would drown to death.

It was his choice.

Carmine was a dead man, no matter what. Johnny and his lowlife family were a loose end for us to tie up.

"Keep going," I told Angelo and then looked at Carmine. "Easy way or the hard way. Doesn't matter to me. We can do this all night."

Carmine was a man of honor, willing to die for a pointless cause. But most men caved under this much pressure. Over the years, I'd learned a lot of torture techniques in this room. The scent of blood, bleach, and death penetrated every inch of the space. They were familiar smells no one should have known by heart.

The abandoned warehouse was like a second home. My father had a rule that if one of us ordered the hit, we executed it as a family.

My childhood was far from average, and my adulthood was even more unusual. When kids my age learned how to ride a bike, my dad taught me how to shoot a gun. I was a perfect shot by the time I was ten years old. With the cold metal in my hand and my finger on the trigger, I felt alive, in control.

I was never more in my element.

Our father raised us to become soldiers in his army. No son of Salvatore Luciano would be anything other than a made man.

I laughed at Angelo for the way he taunted Carmine. Every time I thought Angelo would ease up, he went even harder. My brother loved the thrill of the kill, the high better than sex. Unlike my brother, I saw torture as a means to an end. Though I would have been lying to myself if I didn't admit I occasionally enjoyed a kill.

Some men had it coming to them.

I patted Angelo's shoulder. "Take a break." I hovered over Carmine. "One more chance before I shove that bottle down your fucking throat."

"Fuck you," Carmine spat, water and mucus streaming down his chin.

I drizzled some of the water on Carmine's forehead. A wicked, joker-like grin tipped up the corners of Angelo's mouth as the water ran down Carmine's nose and into his eyes.

This was how he would die.

With my fingers threaded through Carmine's dark curls, I drowned Carmine with the water.

"Where the fuck is Ava Vianelllo?"

Well, technically, she was a Vitale. But no one outside of our family knew the truth about her parentage. That information would put even more of a target on her back.

Carmine shut his eyes and sobbed, overwhelmed by the pain. "She's with Johnny," he muttered.

"Tell me where. Dead or alive, you're not leaving this table until we find her."

But before he could respond, he blacked out.

Chapter Eleven

DANTE

I woke up in less pain than the night before. It was time to go home and get the fuck out of this hospital bed. Ava talked me into it, and I listened only because I knew she was right. Going home would have been mistake.

Nico entered the room with Stefan and Angelo trailing behind him. The twins didn't look like they'd been shot last week.

"Yeah, so…" Angelo sighed, shoving a hand through his black hair. "We got a problem. Vinnie Corallo is working with Johnny Z. He took Ava from the cafeteria."

I winced as I slid my legs off the side of the bed, trying to hide my pain level from my brothers. "Are you fucking kidding me? Vinnie?"

I could barely get out the words.

"Dante, c'mon." Angelo curled his hand around my forearm. "Stop trying to get up. You're going to hurt yourself."

I shook him off. "Don't tell me what to do. I'm the fucking boss."

He scrubbed a hand across the scar on his right cheek, which he often did when stressed. "Yeah, I know."

I paused for a moment. "Tell me what happened to Ava."

"I left Ava in your room to help Paulie plan dad's funeral. I wasn't gone that long."

"Why didn't you put someone on my door?"

"I did," Nico countered. "Tony and Pete were standing watch in the hallway. I guess they didn't see her leave."

"She should have known better." I aimed a hateful stare at the bastard brother. "And you… How could you let this happen, Nicodemus? You had one job. I left you in charge of her safety."

I hated Ava for a long time. Over the past few months, she had grown on me like mold. But now, I couldn't imagine going back to my boring, routine life without her.

She's my queen.

If we found Ava alive, she would one day be my

wife. That was my father's dying wish, one I planned to honor.

"I thought she would be safe here," Nico said with a defeated look. "How was I supposed to know Vinnie was working behind our backs with Johnny Z?"

"He's right," Stefan chimed. "None of us knew. Not even me and I worked with Vinnie every day."

"That's not the worst part," Nico said. "Ava is up for auction. We have less than seven hours to find her."

"You three are fucking idiots. I can't even get shot without you fucking up." I held out my palm. "Where's my phone?"

"Umm…" Angelo turned his head to the side, giving me his scared little boy face. "I don't know."

My brothers thought they were tough, but not with me. They reverted to boys in my presence. The dynamic between us complicated our unusual arrangement with Ava.

"I'll get it." Nico crossed the room and opened a drawer. "Who do you need to call?"

"That's how we find Ava."

His eyebrows tipped up with a question.

"The bracelet I gave Ava for her birthday has a tracking chip." I wiggled my fingers, and he placed the phone in my palm. "I have an app that traces her movements."

"Wow." Angelo chuckled. "Is this what Dante looks

like when he's in love? Crazy stalker."

"I'm not in love," I fired back as I flipped through the apps. "Just keeping tabs on our employees."

"Uh-huh," Stefan grunted. "Do we track all of our employees and give them penthouses and expensive presents?"

"She's more than our employee," Angelo interjected. "Fucking admit it, Dante. You like Ava."

I rolled my eyes and waited for the app to triangulate Ava's exact location. "I like fucking her."

"Well, that's something, I guess." Stefan shook his head and laughed. "But we all know you more than like Ava."

I lifted my head to look at him. "And you do?"

He bobbed his head. "I love her."

"Me, too," Nico added.

I looked at Angelo. "Don't tell me she's got you, too."

Angelo bobbed his head, avoiding my gaze.

"She's going to be my wife," I reminded them.

Angelo snickered. "If she even accepts your lame-ass proposal."

Stefan shifted his stance from one foot to the other. "A marriage changes nothing. Ava is ours."

I glanced at the screen, the hourglass spinning as it tried to locate Ava. "I'm not sharing my wife with my brothers."

Shitty service paired with hospital WiFi wasn't a great combination.

"You don't have a choice," Angelo said with fire behind his words. "Ava belongs to the Kings."

I shared everything with my brothers but never a woman.

Not until now.

"I will allow it," I said to the group. "But there will be rules that all of you will follow."

Nico folded his arms over his chest. "Such as?"

I figured one day they would grow bored of sharing one woman. Angelo and Stefan always liked new and shiny toys and never kept girls around for long. Nico was a romantic and seemed the most in love with her.

Before I could lay down the law with my brothers, a box popped up on the screen with a ding.

"Ava's at a house Brigantine." I showed them the address on my phone and sat up but not without a shit tone of pain. "We're getting her back before the auction ends."

"We?" Angelo shook his head. "No, you're staying right here, big bro."

"The fuck I am," I tossed back at him. "I'm getting back our girl and putting a fucking bullet in Johnny Z's head. And there ain't a damn thing you can do to stop me."

Chapter Twelve

AVA

I awoke in a different room on a dirty mattress pushed against a stone wall. Candles lined the perimeter, leading a path to the door. At least a dozen twin mattresses were on the floor beside me, occupied by sleeping women. With their heads turned to the side, I couldn't tell if they were breathing.

Where am I?

After Johnny's guard locked me in the bedroom, he reappeared with a tray of food and a glass of water. I downed the contents so quickly that the drugs hit me at once. And then, I was floating above my body, high for a moment until I passed out.

So what game was Johnny playing?

I went from his private bedroom down the hall to

what looked like a dingy basement. It smelled moldy and damp, the scent permeating the space.

I sat cross-legged on the mattress with my back against the wall, dressed in lingerie. My heart pounded against my rib cage as if it were clawing its way out of my chest.

A chill raced down my arms as cold air blew through a vent in the ceiling. I ran my hands over my arms and shivered, my teeth chattering.

It was freezing.

Like an arctic blast.

My stomach ached from the hunger pains. Or maybe it was because of all the drugs they had been feeding me. Bile rose from the back of my throat, choking me.

I was thirsty, beyond dehydrated. So when I spotted a water bottle on the floor across the room, I used all my strength to push myself up from the bed. Staggering over to the empty mattress, I plopped down and grabbed the bottle.

Of course, it was empty.

Not a single drop left.

Fuck.

I threw the bottle onto the floor and dragged my tired body over to the door. To my surprise, the knob turned.

It was too good to be true.

This must have been a test, but I had to escape. Nico may have called me *passerotta*, his little sparrow, but I wasn't a bird someone could cage.

I poked my head into the dark hallway.

An overweight man sat in a chair with his hands on his lap. He slept with his head against the wall.

I covered my mouth with my hand, despite my panicked breathing. My lungs were tight, making each intake of breath sharper than the last. Without my inhaler, I had to do everything I could to control my breathing. So far, I had done a decent job, but I could feel it in my lungs that I wouldn't last much longer without my inhaler.

I crept past the man on my tip-toes, careful not to make a sound. He stirred for a moment but didn't open his eyes. I ran down the narrow corridor. The soles of my feet burned as they scraped the cement floor. But I blocked out the pain, willing my body to keep going.

"Hey," the man yelled from behind me.

Shit.

With him on my tail, I didn't bother to look over my shoulder. I couldn't risk losing the lead on him. The closer he got, the muskiness of his cologne filled the cramped space.

When I hit the end of the hall, he closed the distance between us, reaching for my arm. I weaved to the left, rounding a dark corner, and he missed my arm by a few inches. Wires dropped through the exposed ceiling, with wooden planks holding up the insulation. Camping lanterns were placed sporadically along the hall, providing a golden glow.

I turned another corner and spotted a door in front of me.

Yes!

I picked up the pace, my body kicking into overdrive.

Only a few more steps.

Almost there.

I clutched the doorknob with only seconds to spare and swung the door open. The heavy wood hit the man behind me, but that didn't deter him. He grabbed my shoulder and pulled me into his chest.

"You're a feisty little bitch," he growled in my ear, the scent of cigars lifting off his breath. "Time for your punishment."

I wasn't going back to that room.

No fucking way.

So I planted my foot on the wall and threw my body into his. He loosened his grip long enough for me to elbow him in the face.

My jailer let out a deep growl.

I elbowed him again, this time even harder. No one was getting in the way of my freedom.

Not even this fucker.

I made it up a few steps before he grabbed me from behind. Keeping a firm grip on the railing, I kicked him in the dick hard enough to knock him down the stairs.

He groaned when he hit the bottom landing. "You're going to pay for that, bitch."

No, I'm not.

I raced through the door, the man now climbing the stairs behind me. It was so bright upstairs that my eyes hurt from the sudden adjustment. I was like a vampire rising from a coffin in the middle of the day.

The home had a Tuscan vibe, various shades of white and creams, tastefully decorated with modern art. Classy but nothing special. This didn't feel like the home of a sleazeball like Johnny Zabatino. I expected a brothel.

When the man caught up to me again, he yanked on my long hair. I fell backward into his chest, kicking and punching. We dropped to the ground, and my elbow whacked him in the face.

He grunted.

I had the upper hand for a moment and got on top, pinning him to the floor, punching his face with everything I had.

Fuck, my knuckles hurt.

But I had to keep going.

It wasn't easy to land punches, not with him trying

to throw me off him. His hand slipped beneath his suit jacket, and he pulled out a gun.

I reached for the weapon, and a struggle ensued. He was so much bigger than me that his body felt like weights on top of me. I wrapped my legs around his neck when he rolled onto his side. I squeezed so hard his face turned red.

His grip on the gun loosened.

I took it from his hand, unsure about using it. I'd never even held a gun before, and it was much heavier than I had expected.

I got on my knees.

Aimed it at his face.

Pulled the trigger.

And nothing.

Jammed.

I kept trying to shoot.

He clamped his thick arms around me. The asshole wrestled me for the gun, the two of us tumbling across the marble floor. I smacked him with the butt of the weapon.

His weight slowed him down, so I used this to my advantage, even though he was trying to crush me. But I could roll out from under him because I was so much smaller.

I heard footsteps tapping the floor from a distance and panicked. I had to get away from him before the next person tried to capture me. So I hit him with the gun again, and he dropped to the floor, blood dripping from his forehead.

He was down for now, so I got on top of him and bashed his skull with the gun. My arms and hands fucking ached, the pain intensifying with each whack. Blood splashed across my face and got into my eyes.

I closed my mouth and continued to hit him until the footsteps halted in front of me. Four sets of shiny, black dress shoes.

I glanced up and breathed a sigh of relief.

Angelo ran his knuckles across his jaw, stripping me bare with his eyes. "Anyone else hard as fuck right now?"

Stefan, Nico, and Dante stood at his side. A large group of men in suits were behind them. The Luciano brothers made guttural sounds in answer to Angelo's question.

They stared at me with equal parts desire and fascination. Dante looked like he was going to devour me. Although I could see that he was in pain, clutching his side for comfort. He would never voice his concern aloud.

Nico stepped out from the group and shrugged off his jacket, holding it out for me. "*Vieni, passerrota.* No one is going to hurt you."

I slid off the dead man, the gun still in my hand. "Took you long enough to find me."

A frown pulled at Nico's mouth. "We haven't stopped looking for you since Vinnie took you." He put his jacket over my shoulders and pulled it closed. "We don't have long before we have to shoot our way out of here."

"I killed him," I choked out.

He glanced at the man and smiled. "Impressive. Tommy Bones was one of Johnny Z's top hitmen." He took the gun from my hand and glanced at it. "You could've saved yourself a lot of trouble if you turned off the safety."

I nearly collapsed from exhaustion, and he lifted me off the floor. "Is that why it didn't work?"

Nico nodded. "Remind me to show you how to shoot when we get home." He stroked my hair with his fingers and hugged me. "I got you, *passerrota*." He kissed my forehead and whispered, "It's going to be okay." His eyes dropped to my lack of clothing, and he shook his head. "Did they hurt you?"

"No. But they drugged me a few times."

He brushed the pad of his thumb over my bottom lip and bent down to kiss my forehead.

"Enough, lover boy," Dante said from behind us. "Let's go before you get me shot. Again."

Chapter Thirteen

AVA

We ran from the mansion before the auction ended. Gunshots fired behind us as we left the property, just missing us. The five of us piled into the back of a van driven by Tony. It was dark outside, but I could see the Luciano brothers' faces with the moonlight entering through the back window.

Dante's cell phone beeped with a new message. "They got Johnny Z and Vinnie."

"What about Paulie?" I asked.

Dante grinned like a psychopath. "We're saving him for last."

"What if he runs when he finds out you have Johnny and Vinnie? One of them will rat him out."

"We stick to the plan," Dante said in a firm tone.

"After my father's funeral, Paulie is a dead man. Not a second sooner."

Since Dante was always in charge, I bobbed my head. He'd been planing his revenge all week in the hospital. And after those assholes kidnapped me, I bet he wanted to get even more than before.

Nico moved me between his spread thighs and ran his hands up and down my skin. It felt so fucking good I moaned. Dante sat across from us, staring between my legs like he had X-ray vision. I could feel the heat of his gaze on every inch of my body. My skin sizzled from the fire brewing inside me.

I was a different person.

A murderer.

Killing that man was the final straw. I felt the darkness clawing at my heart, draining all of the good from my soul. Maybe I was always supposed to be with made men. From the start, I couldn't stay away from them.

Now, I never wanted to leave.

The Boardwalk Kings were mine.

I leaned back on Nico's chest and spread my legs for Dante. Stefan sat on Dante's right, also staring at me. Angelo was on his left, glaring at me like an animal ready to attack.

Nico curled his arm around me and kissed my neck. "Stop teasing my brothers, or they won't think twice about bending you over and fucking you." He nibbled on my earlobe. "Do you want my brothers to fuck you? Huh, my little cock slut?"

I turned around to straddle him, unzipped his pants, and put him inside me. "They can watch me fuck you first."

He grabbed my ass and impaled me with his massive cock.

"Oh, God." I breathed hard against his lips. "Nico, fuck me."

I ripped off Nico's jacket and the white T-shirt. With my back to his brothers, they had the perfect view as Nico's dick drove in and out of me.

Nico was so big that he stretched me out. I bit my lip, which he took between his teeth.

"What did I tell you about biting that lip?

I heard one of my men move behind me, then strong hands gripped my hips and pulled me off Nico.

"Hey," I yelled.

"Shut your mouth," Dante growled.

He turned me around so my back faced Nico and helped me ride his brother. Then he unzipped his pants and whipped out his big dick. "You never know when to stop talking, do you?" Dante stroked his long length and smacked my lips with the tip. "So I'm gonna keep this pretty mouth occupied."

With his hand on my head, he shoved his dick past

my lips while Nico fucked me. My God, this was hot. I was so wet my juices leaked out of me and onto Nico.

He gripped my hips and slammed into me, finding a rhythm with Dante. His hand rubbed my thigh. "Take it like a good girl." Nico dragged his teeth across my neck, pumping into me. "You like taking two dicks at the same time?"

I nodded, moaning with Dante yanking on my scalp, fucking my mouth.

"She's a good little whore," Dante said to Nico. His eyes met mine as my cheeks puffed out from him. "Suck my cock, *puttana*." His fingers wove through my hair, pulling hard enough to make me scream. "Hurry up and cum, Nicodemus. Her pussy is mine."

As I sucked on Dante, I noticed Stefan and Angelo on the other side of the van with their dicks hanging out of their pants.

Angelo spat into his hand and ran it up and down his shaft. Stefan was already rubbing cock raw, watching us like a live porno. Nico's fingers burrowed into my ass as he stretched me out, thrusting deeper.

I hummed on Dante's cock, and he looked down at me, his chest rising and falling.

After Nico came inside me, Dante stepped back, his cock in front of my face, covered with my spit. He reached down and lifted me off Nico, then bent me over. My knees hurt from the hard floor of the van.

Dante turned me to face his brothers and grabbed my hips.

"Look at how wet you are for us."

I stared at Nico, Stefan, and Angelo on my hands and knees while their brother dominated me. Dante spanked me like a rotten child, one after the other, and it felt so damn good. A mixture of Nico's cum and my juices slid down my thighs.

"Hit me harder, Daddy." I glanced over my shoulder at him and smirked. "I've been a bad girl."

"Yeah, you have." His eyes flickered with excitement and a hint of madness. "Little brat." He fisted my hair in one hand and slapped my ass with the other. Then he entered me from behind in one quick thrust, filling me. "Fuck, your pussy is so tight."

It hurt at first, but as he punished me, the pain eventually became pleasurable. Nico was hard again and stroking himself. Angelo and Stefan had already stripped down, still touching themselves. They hadn't come yet. So I assumed they were waiting for their turn.

I moaned for Dante as he wrecked my body. After days of forced captivity, my entire body ached. My legs and pussy were so sore that I wasn't sure how I would handle the twins.

Dante slid his hand beneath my chin so my eyes were on his brothers. He wanted them to watch us.

Each time Dante's thick cock pushed between my wet folds, I closed my eyes and breathed through my nose. He fucked me so hard my stomach brushed the floor as he thrust his hips.

Moans tumbled out of my mouth, turning into screams. He enjoyed punishing me, and I loved every second of it.

He squeezed my shoulder and fucked me like a possessed demon. Our skin slapped, his balls hitting me from how hard he entered me. I screamed his name until I couldn't speak anymore.

Unlike Nico, Dante didn't give me a second to adjust to his size. He kept pounding into me like he was trying to mold his cock into my vagina. I came once, twice, until I lost count.

Dante came and collapsed on top of me.

The second after Dante pulled out, Angelo dragged me over to him and flipped me onto my back. He rolled his tongue over my aching clit, ripping a whimper from my lips. I arched my back, needing more of his tongue.

He devoured me, taking turns between sucking on my clit and licking between my folds. I gripped the ends of his black hair and pulled, screaming his name. He lifted my thigh and dropped it over his shoulder, sliding two fingers inside me to coat his fingers with cum.

When I screamed again, Stefan was in front of me, shoving his dick between my lips.

Angelo peeked at me from between my thighs, my cum glistening on his lips. He gave me one of his sadistic smiles that would have terrified other women. Then he ravaged me, tasting me as if he would never eat again.

As I hit the peak of my climax, Stefan wrapped his long fingers around my throat and squeezed. His legs trembled, and then his cum filled my mouth a moment later.

He pulled out and wiped his thumb across my bottom lip. "Swallow all of me."

Angelo climbed on top of me and sucked my nipple into his mouth. He bit and played with the tiny bud for a second, and then he was straddling my head, pushing his cock into my mouth. His lips parted as our eyes met, forcing me to take all of him.

So I sucked, ignoring the pain as he gripped my hair like he wanted to rip it from my scalp.

"Fuck," he grunted.

I gagged with him so far down my throat, and he seemed to get the hint that he was fucking my mouth like a savage.

"Suck my cock, dirty girl." Angelo tugged on the ends of my hair. "Oh, fuck. You're so good at that."

I opened my mouth wide as he shot his cum on my

tongue, some dripping down my chin. He slid down my body, and with a sick grin, he licked my lips.

Even though I wanted him to kiss me, he didn't. Angelo continued his slow exploration of my lips and chin, lapping up our cum.

And then he surprised me by saying, "I missed you, *dolcezza*."

Chapter Fourteen

DANTE

Getting shot changes a lot of shit. It gave me a new perspective on life and a different way of viewing myself and the world. Of course, the doctor wasn't thrilled about me leaving the hospital without medical clearance. But when you're Dante Luciano and run this fucking city, you can do whatever you want.

So the doc would come to us.

He was our new employee.

The five of us entered my penthouse and headed straight into the kitchen. My place was an open concept with bedrooms on the first and second floors and a large patio overlooking the Atlantic Ocean.

I loved my apartment.

This was the only place where I felt at peace, apart

from the casino floor. I could lower my guard inside these walls and not worry about keeping up appearances.

I pointed my finger at the barstool and gestured for Ava to sit. Stefan was faster than me and pulled out the stool for her.

Ava sat between Angelo and Stefan. There was no separating the three of them. Despite not wanting to share with my brothers, I had no choice. I was stuck with this ridiculous arrangement.

Until death do us part.

Nico moved behind me as I opened the refrigerator, placing his hand on my shoulder. "Let me cook, Dante."

I shook off his hand. "I'm fully capable of making a meal for us."

"No one said you're not. But you need to take it easy." His hand slid to my upper back in some weird ass motion meant to soothe me, but it only pissed me off more. "Let me do this."

"No." I walked away from him and placed the carton of eggs on the counter. "Sit."

"You're going to rip out your stitches." He flung out his hand, nostrils flared. "None of you were supposed to leave the fucking hospital. But you think you know better than the doctors."

I reached into the drawer for two pans and set

them on the stove, biting the inside of my cheek to keep from screaming. Excruciating pain radiated up my side, spreading down my leg.

I knew he was right.

But did I care?

Not a chance.

I wasn't in shape to be standing in the kitchen. But my girl needed to eat. It was my responsibility to take care of the family, including Ava.

She was one of us.

"I'm not staying in a disgusting room, sleeping on a flat pillow, or wearing a fucking hospital gown for one more night," I told Nico. "So get off my ass about leaving the hospital. The doctor will be here tomorrow to check on us."

"Someone needs to change all your dressings," he shot back.

"I can do it," Ava offered. "I know what to do."

I angled my body to look at her, one eyebrow raised.

"My mom had surgery when I was ten," she explained. "The nurse showed me how to change her dressings. I remember how to do it."

"We're grown men," I told her.

"That doesn't mean you can't take our help." She shot up from the chair and slowly approached me.

"The three of you could have died. And you left the hospital against the doctor's orders to find me."

"I would do it again," I said with my eyes on her. She was so fucking beautiful, even with dirt on her skin, mascara staining her tanned cheeks. "So would my brothers."

Stefan and Angelo grunted in agreement.

Ava stared at me with those big brown eyes. "I can't lose you, Dante. Waiting to see if you would wake up was the worst kind of torture. So will you please let Nico cook for us?"

I held her gaze for a long moment. "If it will make you happy."

She beamed with a smile that lit up her face. "It will make me very happy." Standing on her tippy toes, she reached up to kiss my lips. I kissed her back, a quick peck that seemed to satisfy her. "Come sit with me at the dining room table." Ava wiggled her fingers. "Please."

I took her hand and raised it to my lips, kissing her soft skin. A bright smile touched her pretty eyes that didn't leave mine, not even for a second.

I never thought I would feel anything for anyone other than my brothers. But this girl was breaking down my walls brick by brick, forcing me to let her into my world. A part of me hated it because that meant being vulnerable. And I didn't have room in my life for weaknesses.

"I want waffles," Ava said to Nico before guiding me by the hand over to the dining room table. "And bacon."

"Me, too," Stefan chimed.

"I'll take an omelet," Angelo added.

"Dante?" Nico said with a question in his tone.

I hooked my arm around her slim waist and pulled her onto the dining chair with me. "Same as Ava."

She slid her arm across my neck and planted kisses on my cheeks. I didn't hate her touch anymore. Now, I liked the feel of her skin pressed against mine, the warmth of her breath on my cheek.

I loved everything about her.

It wasn't her body or that beautiful face that attracted me to her. I liked how her mind worked. She was an intelligent girl, and I respected people with unique gifts. My dad used to say I had an eye for talent, and I was the one who suggested he bring Ava to Atlantic City.

It was an idea I had tossed out over a glass of scotch one night in his parlor. We knew Giancarlo was stealing from us and couldn't prove it. And after seeing Ava at the mayor's party with her father, I got the idea to recruit her. It was inevitable with her father laundering our money and her being so skilled with investing.

I let everyone think it was my dad's idea. After all, he was the boss of the family. But I planted the seed in his mind until, eventually, the plan came to fruition. I'd always been curious about her and wondered if she would be helpful to us.

Ava was no longer a pawn.

She was mine.

Ours.

Her lips brushed mine, soft and gentle, opposite what I liked. Although, when it came to Ava, my tastes were changing. I would always enjoy rough, kinky sex. But with her, I wanted to be different, somewhere in between.

"I'm glad you're okay," Ava said in a hushed tone. "I meant what I said, Dante. We need you."

I grabbed the back of her head and kissed her, parting her lips with my tongue. This time, the kiss lasted until the air drained from my lungs. And when our lips separated, I blurted out the first thing that came to mind.

"Marry me."

Eyes wide, she gasped. "What?"

"You heard me, good girl." I slid my hand beneath her chin, feeling her pulse pounding. "Marry me."

"What the fuck?" Angelo shouted, the legs of the wooden stool scraping across the tiled floor as he got up. "You can't ask Ava to marry you without us."

"Yeah," Stefan said with a groan. "This is a team effort, big bro."

"Not quite," I said to correct him.

"I'm with the twins," Nico said to add his two cents. "We're in this together."

They were so fucking annoying.

All three of them.

Deal or not, I didn't owe them anything. But for some idiotic reason, I felt they were right about this. Ava wasn't letting any of us go, and my brothers were too stupid in love to walk away.

Ava shifted her weight on my lap and licked her lips. "Why do you want to marry me?"

"Because it was my father's dying wish."

At least, it was the truth.

Not the best answer, though.

A slight frown tugged at Ava's mouth. "I want you to want to marry me."

I tightened my grip on her hip and pulled her closer. "I do."

"I want to marry for love," she whispered.

"You love me." I yanked on her hair and kissed her pink lips. "I know you do. So marry me."

"But I want you to love me."

What I felt for Ava was something.

Was it love?

Maybe.

I had no fucking clue what it felt like to be in love with someone. I never had a girlfriend or allowed myself to get close to a woman. Until Ava, I hadn't even fucked a woman while looking at her.

Never even kissed.

I didn't need intimacy from the women I screwed. They were there for my entertainment and enjoyment. Their needs never mattered to me.

I paid them and left.

A simple transaction.

"Do you think you'll ever love me?" Ava rested her forehead against mine, awaiting my answer.

I breathed harder as I considered her question, hating how my heart beat faster when she looked directly at me. She had the strangest effect on my body. Something I never felt with another person.

Only her.

"Yes."

She gave me a tiny smile. "What about your brothers?"

"What about them?"

"You have to make room for them in our married life."

"They're not going anywhere," I assured her.

"Then, yes." Her lips touched mine. "I'll marry you, Dante."

Chapter Fifteen

STEFAN

After we fed Ava enough food for an army, I led her upstairs and into the bathroom, turning the shower knobs until the water was at the correct temperature.

"I'm so glad you're okay. That you're alive." I got on my knees and stripped off her panties. "I thought I was going to lose my fucking mind."

Ava threaded her fingers through my hair. "I never lost hope you would find me."

With each kiss, I whispered I was sorry and promised never to let her out of my sight. Most of all, I vowed to keep her safe. No one would ever touch the hair on her head again. I would kill anyone who tried to harm Ava.

We got into the shower, and I appraised every inch of her sexy body. She closed her eyes when the water splashed across her beautiful face. When she opened her eyes, she smiled at me. It was the same smile she'd given me the last time I saw her. Still the same girl I was falling in love with for the past few months.

I pulled her slim body against mine, and she wrapped her arms around me, leaning her head on my chest. "I thought I lost you."

"You could never lose me, Stefan." She moved her hand up my chest to cover my heart. "Because I will always be in here."

I stroked her cheek. "*Cuore mio.*"

This was real love—the kind of love worth fighting for.

Worth dying for.

She was my heart, my soul.

I leaned against the tiled wall and cupped her breast, massaging her nipple with my thumb. As always, Ava was responsive to my touch. The tiny bud hardened for me, and she moaned softly. I just wanted to touch her, make sure she was real.

We stayed that way for a while. There wasn't anything sexual about it.

When our skin started to prune, I lifted a bottle of shampoo and washed her hair, then rubbed body wash on her skin. I lathered the soap in my hands and rubbed it down her arms, taking my time when I got to her chest. Ava covered my hands with hers and held them over her breasts.

She licked her lips, drinking in some of the water that landed on her face. "I want you, Stefan."

I brushed my lips along her ear. "After you get some sleep and recover, you will feel me everywhere."

She shook her head. "I don't want to wait. My body might be sore from the drugs and the shitty conditions, but I need this. Go slow. Be gentle. Take your time. Show me how much you've missed me."

I kissed her, soft and sensual for once. Each kiss was a silent promise as I made love to her mouth.

Ava slid her hands up to my neck and hooked her leg around me, digging her heel into my ass. I lifted her, and she dragged her fingers down my arms, her nails piercing my skin. I liked the pain. Feeling something with Ava made all of this real.

She was mine.

I wasn't letting her go.

Ever.

When you have something worth fighting for, you must protect it at all costs. Ava was it for me. No one and nothing could ever compare to her. She absolved me of my sins and forgave me when I was at my worst.

Gripping Ava by the hips, I lowered her onto my cock and used the wall for support. She pressed down on my shoulders, her tits bouncing in my face. I opened my mouth and took her nipple between my teeth, pulling out of her slowly before I filled her up again.

She screamed my name, her voice growing louder. Ava was so close I could feel her pussy milking my cock. I wasn't too far behind her.

She was too tight, too warm, and her body too perfect for me to focus on anything else. I couldn't distract myself. I wanted to get lost in her, feel every inch of her.

Ava came so hard that her orgasm rocked through me. She moaned. I growled, biting her nipple harder as I came along with her.

Out of breath, I peeled my mouth from her breast and looked at her. "I love you, *bellezza*." I set her on the floor. "So fucking much."

"I love you, too." She smiled and placed her palm on my chest. "Thank you for saving me."

I shook my head and sighed. "I didn't save you. I couldn't even find you without Dante's help."

I felt worthless for not being the one to bring Ava back safely. That was my job, and I failed.

"You saved me in other ways." She spoke so low it was hard to hear her over the water beating on my back. "When I was starting to lose hope, I thought of you. I knew we would find our way back to each other."

I kissed her lips. "My queen."

Ava smiled against my lips. "My king."

Chapter Sixteen

DANTE

After Ava showered with Stefan, she exited my bathroom with a towel wrapped around her slim waist. I lay on top of the comforter, shoes off, feet dangling off the edge of the bed, and raised my hand to beckon her.

A seductive look spread across her beautiful face as she dropped the bath towel on the floor. I sat up and appraised every inch of her body.

Fuck, she looked good enough to eat.

When I asked her to marry me, I wasn't sure if she would say yes. But when we locked eyes, I felt a spark. Palpable energy that made the air between us crackle with electricity. I'd felt a connection to Ava from the start.

My sexy girl got on the bed, kneeling beside me.

Without a word, I massaged her nipple, the tiny bud hardening from my touch. We didn't have to speak to communicate. She always seemed to know what I liked, what I needed.

Stefan hadn't spoken a word. He stood in the entryway to the bathroom, naked and drying his hair with a towel. Ava's eyes flicked between us.

She wet her lips with her tongue. "Stefan, come here."

Then her gaze shifted to me, expecting me to protest. But my expression hadn't changed. Now that she was ours, we would give her whatever she wanted. And if she wanted to fuck all of us, then so be it.

Ava grabbed my hand and inched it up her thigh. Stefan gave me a look as if he were asking for permission.

My brother got on the mattress beside her and tilted her head back. "Is this what you want, *bellezza*?"

She placed both of our hands on her inner thighs. "Yes."

Ava gripped our wrists and moved our hands to her big tits, helping us massage her nipples. We let her lead the way, even though we were used to taking charge in the bedroom.

This was all new to me.

Like Nico, I never shared a woman with my brothers. Never shared a woman with anyone. It was never more than a business transaction until Ava disrupted my life.

I glanced at Stefan, who waited for me to nod my approval. He didn't waste a second and bent down and sucked Ava's nipple into his mouth. Stefan made her squirm with each flick of his tongue.

She moaned and yanked on my boxers. Impatient and greedy, she was ravenous, like she couldn't wait another second.

"Get naked," she grunted, her eyes meeting mine.

"Didn't get enough of us on the way home?" I smirked and pushed on her shoulder, dragging her down to the mattress. "Sit back and let us take care of you."

I was too sore to fuck her the way I did in the van. Stefan's injuries weren't as bad as mine, but he looked fucking spent. The trip to Johnny's house had taken a lot of us.

Ava licked her lips, then grabbed Stefan's hair, tugging at the ends. He stuck out his tongue and peeked at her as he licked her nipple. Ava whimpered when he did it again, teasing her.

"Stefan," she whispered with a handful of his hair between her fingers. "I missed you." Then her eyes fell on me. "I missed you, too, Dante."

As our eyes met, I tucked a strand of hair behind her ear, breathing against her lips. A rush of heat coursed through my veins and spread down my arms. I pulled her mouth to mine, kissing her lips as Stefan kissed her neck.

"Dante," she moaned as I peppered her jaw with kisses. "Stefan," she groaned when he rolled his tongue along her neck.

We took turns licking and sucking on her skin, and my pretty girl trembled with need. I clutched her chin and forced her to look into my eyes. Stefan slid his hand up her stomach and massaged her breasts, nibbling on her earlobe as I swept my tongue into her mouth.

I pinched her nipple, and she screamed out in pleasure.

"Feel good?"

She closed her eyes and breathed through her nose. "Don't stop."

I inched down her body and sucked her nipple into my mouth. Stefan covered the right side of her body in kisses, working in unison with me.

I should have hated the sight of his hands, mouth, and tongue on my future wife. But after everything we'd been through, I didn't care that he loved her.

Or that she loved him.

We were a family.

She grabbed my hand and moved it lower. "Dante, please."

Ava rocked her hips, her hand falling to the back of my head, begging me to touch her. So I thrust my fingers inside her. She was tight and wet, so ready for me.

I was dying to be inside her, but this was about making her feel good. And I knew my injuries had limits. I'd already pushed myself too far.

As I fucked her with my fingers, moans slipped from her throat. Stefan kissed her lips as I moved between her thighs. Ava arched her back, lifting her hips off the mattress. She moaned into Stefan's mouth as I devoured her.

Her eyes slammed shut when I sucked her clit into my mouth. I licked between her slick folds, desperate to taste every inch of her. My good girl tugged on the ends of my hair, screaming my name.

I'd never done this before. I never even thought about licking a woman's pussy. But Ava tasted as good as she looked.

She was my favorite addiction.

Rocking her hips, she strangled me with her pussy. Whimpers poured out of her mouth, and her legs trembled. One after another, she rode out her orgasms, coming on my tongue.

I sat up, staring at her from between her spread thighs. Stefan rested his hand on her thigh, his eyes on her naked body. I cleared my throat, and his gaze drifted between us.

Ava covered her hand with her mouth and yawned.

I tugged on her hair. "Tired?"

She nodded.

I rolled onto my side of the bed. Stefan was on his knees, panting and staring at us. My brother was so used to me issuing orders. He looked like he didn't know what to do or where to go. Like a lost puppy.

Ava laid her head back on the pillows. She grabbed my hand, then Stefan's, and held our hands against the mattress at her sides.

"Stay with us," she whispered to Stefan.

Stefan glanced at me to confirm.

I nodded.

Why the fuck not?

The twins slept with me when they were kids and had nightmares. This wasn't the same. But it wouldn't kill me to let Stefan stay the night if it made our queen happy.

I was exhausted from the day's events and rolled onto my back, staring at the ceiling. A pain shot down my side, and I bit the inside of my cheek. Ava curled up beside me, her head on my chest.

Stefan lay on the other side, his head on the pillow and his hand on Ava's thigh.

She glanced at me and covered my hand with hers. "I can't wait to be your wife."

I hooked my good arm around her, brushing my fingers down her arm. "Get some sleep, Mrs. Luciano."

Her eyes lit up. "I like the sound of that."

Me too.

Chapter Seventeen

NICO

It was hard to say goodbye to the man who gave me life. Dad never made me feel like I was his bastard. But because of everyone else's stupid opinions, I tried to live up to the Luciano name.

I wanted to prove them wrong.

To make my dad proud.

I clutched my mother's hand, standing in front of my father's casket. The funeral home did an excellent job with his makeup and made him look like the man I had admired my entire life.

He was gone.

My dad was the one person in this family that made me feel welcome. I never felt out of place with him. Until recently, Dante and the twins made me feel like I didn't belong. Because of that, I tried to spend as much time away from home as possible. I intentionally chose a college away from home to give me some distance from them.

I wondered if my dad brought Ava into our lives because he knew she would unite us. That we would need each other once he was gone. He had a sixth sense with that kind of stuff. Salvatore Luciano was successful in business and life because he could read people. He always seemed to know what people needed.

"Nico," Mom whimpered, her body shaking as I held her in my arms. "I can't do this."

I smoothed my hand down her back. "Yes, you can, Ma. You're strong. Never needed a man to make your life better."

"I needed your father." Tears streaked down her pale cheeks, staining her skin with black mascara. "He was my rock. And now..."

"Ma, you still have me. You've done just fine on your own all these years."

"Oh, Sal." She placed her hand over her heart, gazing at my father's lifeless face. With her other hand, she touched my father's folded hands. "I knew I shouldn't have left this time. I could see that he needed me. But I had to..." Her voice trailed off from crying so hard, the words muffled.

"Ma, listen to me." I bent down and gripped her shoulders. "There's nothing you could have done to change the outcome of this situation. Being here instead of Vegas wouldn't have made a difference."

"He wasn't himself." Mom laid her head on my chest and sobbed. "I could tell something was wrong."

"Paulie did this to him," I said in a hushed tone. "Not you. And I promise he will pay for every last sin."

My words put a tiny smile on her face. "He deserves a painful death for what he did to your father and your brothers." Her eyes shifted to Paulie, who spoke to Dante in the front row.

"In due time," I assured her. "They will all pay for their betrayal."

"I worry about you, Nico." She tried to curl her fingers around my bicep, but her hand was so small in comparison. "This city is dangerous."

"I'm a Luciano. People fear us." I hugged her. "We're the danger."

After the funeral, our closest friends and family returned to my father's apartment to celebrate his life. Dad believed in remembering how someone lived, not how they died.

After his wife's murder, my dad honored her every Sunday by helping Dante make her favorite meals. It became our weekly ritual, something the twins had grown accustomed to over the years. Dante still cooked for us every Sunday. That would probably never change. Cooking soothed him.

We each had coping mechanisms, ways that we survived our brutal upbringing. Our father had prepared us well. And now that he was gone, the four of us had finally come together. Even Dante was treating me like his brother instead of a stranger.

A group of men hovered around Dante, paying respect to the new boss, swearing their loyalty to the new king of the boardwalk.

Ava latched onto Stefan and Angelo's arms as they led her into the formal dining room. The last time she was in this room, she thought we would kill her.

Dante grabbed a glass of scotch and stood in the center of the dining room. He tapped the glass with a knife to gain everyone's attention. Silence fell over the room.

He raised the glass. "My father was a man of few words. But he had one last request." Dante beckoned Ava with his finger, and she rushed over to him. He slipped his free hand between hers and raised their joined hands. "He wanted me to marry a Vitale."

It was time to put our beef to rest. Our dad was right about uniting with the Vitales. There was no point in tearing apart the city anymore.

"The night of my father's murder, we met to discuss my marriage to Ava, Vincenzo Vitale's daughter."

Dante didn't bother to wait for the chatter to die down before he said, "Ava and I are getting married at the end of the month." His gaze moved to Vincenzo Vitale. "From one boss to another, I'd like your blessing to marry Ava."

My brother should have asked before he put his mother's ring on her finger. But Dante was never one to follow the rules.

Vincenzo stepped out from the group of Vitales. "You have it." He raised his glass. "*Salute.*"

"*Salute,*" everyone said in unison.

My mom clung to my side, tugging on my arm. "I thought you were in love with her."

"I am," I whispered.

"But Ava is going to be your brother's wife."

I laughed. "I'm not even going to bother to explain, Ma. We have an agreement that works for all of us."

She rolled her shoulders and drank the champagne

in her hand. "I'm not one to judge. Look at my relationship with your father. As long as you're happy."

"I'm happy, Ma."

My mom flashed a set of pearly white teeth and smiled. "That's all that matters."

Chapter Eighteen

DANTE

I grinned so fucking much my face hurt. We had Johnny Z strung up by his ankles, shirtless, and his hands tied behind his back. A handkerchief covered his mouth. Tears streamed down his reddened cheeks.

The more he tried to kick and shake free from his shackles, the more energy he wasted.

I laughed.

At least he wasn't a fucking pussy.

I had to give him that.

Most men would have crumbled in this situation. Some even begged for mercy.

But not Johnny Zabatino.

He thought he was invincible.

Standing before him, with a wicked smirk plastered on my face, I tugged the fabric away from his mouth.

"Let me down, you piece of shit," he yelled.

I crossed my arms over my chest and laughed.

Angelo stood at my side, a sharpened blade in his hand and the same evil grin crossing his lips. We had used this tactic dozens of times. With the blood rushing to Johnny Z's head, it wouldn't be long after Angelo sliced him open before he lost consciousness. So even though I wanted my vengeance, I let Angelo do the honors.

Angelo dragged the knife along Johnny's chest. A trail of blood ran down his body, over his right shoulder, and onto the floor. I wanted to cut into his flesh until every last drop of his blood pooled on the floor at my feet.

"You sick fucks," Johnny growled. "You will pay for this. Mark my words."

He closed his eyes for a second and breathed through his nose.

"Don't waste your breath, Zabatino," I shot back. "Dead men don't talk."

Glancing at Angelo, I tilted my head to instruct him to keep going. This time, Angelo stuck the knife into his neck, slicing deeper than before. Blood dripped onto the cement floor, right in front of my Ferragamo oxfords. I took a step back, careful not to ruin my dress shoes.

"Paulie betrayed you." Johnny could barely get out

the words. "And you welcomed him back into the family. Some boss you are."

I kicked him in the face, and his body rocked from side to side. "What did I tell you about opening your fucking mouth?"

He spoke with one eye open, kicking his feet to try to shake free. "You have no power over me. Do your worst, Luciano. My men will come for you. You're too stupid to see the cracks within your ranks."

"For someone tied up and bleeding to death, you still think you hold all the cards." I hunched down next to him and gripped his black hair. "You killed my father. And I'm going to kill you and everyone who helped you."

Angelo had a greedy look in his eyes. Stefan stood off to the side with Ava on his arm. Nico was on her other side, stroking his fingers through her hair. A terrified expression tugged at her pretty face.

But I insisted she watch.

She was about to become our queen. It was only right she stood at our sides and witnessed the demise of our enemies.

I pushed myself up from the floor and brushed my hands down the front of my slacks. "See you in the afterlife, *pompinaro*."

Johnny sucked in a sharp breath. "Just kill me and get it over with already."

"We're not going to kill you tonight." I smirked as his eyes widened. "It will take days for you to bleed out. The slow and painful death you deserve."

I'd always enjoyed killing people.

When I was a teenager, my father brought me to this room and explained the importance of protecting our legacy. He showed me how to maim and torture men until they begged for death. Over the next few days, Johnny would do just that. And I would love every second of it.

He closed his eyes and kept them shut. Blood ran down his chest and neck, still dripping onto the floor. As expected, he lost consciousness.

"Vinnie is next," Stefan said with a bite to his tone. "And he's mine."

I nodded. "He was one of your guys. You should execute him."

Stefan gave me an appreciative look but didn't speak. We had all agreed on the ways we would torture our enemies.

I walked over to Ava and held out my palm. She slipped her fingers between mine, breathing hard.

"It's okay to be afraid." I pulled her to my chest. "But this is how we do business."

Ava covered her mouth with her hand, turning her head away from me.

"What's wrong?"

"The smell." Her nose scrunched. "It's turning my stomach."

"Get used to it, my queen. This won't be the last time you're in this room."

"It stinks of death and bleach. I can't…"

She moved across the room and puked on the floor, her body shaking from the action. Nico was the first to react and held her in his arms, stroking his fingers down her back. I didn't know how to console a person. But Nico was good at it.

I moved beside her and inspected her face, wiping the spit from her mouth with my handkerchief. "You've been sick a lot lately."

"Yeah," she breathed. "I think the drugs messed up my stomach. They knocked me out a bunch of times. Who knows what they gave me."

I glanced at Nico, who had a concerned look on his face. Without words, I could tell we were thinking the same thing. Our father was only in the ground for a few days.

But with death comes life.

Angelo cleaned the blood off his hands and walked over to us with Stefan at his side. "Everything okay, pretty girl?"

She shook her head. "I don't feel good."

Angelo tucked her hair behind her ears. "Are you still taking your pills?"

She shook her head. "No, not since before Vinnie kidnapped me."

Nico's face lit up with a smile. "I think you're pregnant."

"No." She waved her hand to dismiss the idea. "I can't be. We have too much going on. It's not a good time."

Stefan laughed. "That's not how this works. You don't get to pick and choose."

Ava bit her lip, her eyes finding mine. "But I'm marrying Dante. I can't be pregnant."

I raised my hand to beckon her. She inched forward until our chests pressed together. Her body trembled as if she feared my response to the situation. I wasn't mad. The thought of her possibly carrying my child excited me.

"You looked scared." I clutched her shoulder. "Don't be. I'm not mad. This is a good thing. We'll figure it out as a family."

Chapter Nineteen

STEFAN

I learned how to swing a baseball bat when I was five. The old man took me down to the park with my brothers under the pretense I had a shot at being something other than a Wiseguy. Back then, I'd wanted to be many things—a baseball player, a Marine, a cowboy, and even a cop.

I thought I had a choice.

I thought I had a future.

But mine was chosen for me.

Not until I was older did I realize why Papa took us down to the park. It wasn't to learn how to hit a home run. It was to show us how to inflict pain.

How to be a Luciano.

Every life lesson had a purpose.

Papa didn't do anything half-assed.

I took a step back with the bat clutched between my fingers, my grip so tight my bones hurt. Then, I swung like my father had shown me, sending Vinnie to the ground with one hit. I stood over him and slammed the metal into his back.

"How could you?" I couldn't stop myself from hitting him again, the pain and anger taking hold of me. "You fucking piece of shit."

Blood seeped from his mouth as he rolled onto his side and covered his head with his hands.

I could only see my father taking his last breath when the bat's tip landed between Vinnie's eyes. Rage burned inside me, fueled by my need for revenge.

I was a Luciano.

A soldier.

A man who couldn't see past his pain.

Crack—there went his ribs.

Another crack—split open his head.

I couldn't stop myself.

Vinnie's blood splashed on my face and hair, some of it staining my brand new suit. When I wasn't hitting Vinnie with the bat, I kicked him with the tip of my dress shoe. He was one of the men I trusted most, and I treated him like a brother. So, fuck him, and fuck his stupid face.

I whacked him again, this time harder than the last. His skin was covered in blood, his face swollen and bloody beyond recognition. Dante, of all people, had to pull me back from Vinnie's limp body. He was long past dead, and I didn't feel any better.

I felt nothing.

"That's enough, baby bro." Dante tightened his arms around me. "He's gone."

"Let me go. Let me fucking go, Dante!" I elbowed him in the stomach and broke free from his grasp. I spun around to face him, the bat at my side and my teeth clenched in anger. "You don't understand."

He closed the gap between us, his mouth twisted in disgust. "I know exactly how you feel, Stef."

I threw the bat on the ground, hitting Vinnie with it one last time.

Fucking traitor.

He deserved every broken bone.

That piece of shit had earned a bloody death at my hand. Vinnie turned his back on the family.

We were at the same spot in the woods where we took Ava to scare her into telling us the truth. This was our usual dump site for our victims. She stood beside Nico with her head turned away from the bloody stump that was once Vinnie Corallo. Even Angelo looked slightly disgusted, which was saying something.

I gave Vinnie a good kick in the ribs to roll him over and into the grave that I made him dig before I beat him to death. I had his blood on my shoes and clothes, some on my face. If I could have killed him again, I would have.

But it wouldn't bring my dad back.

"Paulie is next," I said to Dante.

Arms crossed over his suit-clad chest, he nodded.

We hadn't spoken much over the past few hours. All of us had vengeance in our hearts and blood on our hands. We had nothing to talk about until we put our father's killers into the ground.

Paulie and three others were digging their graves. They were beaten to a pulp, their faces almost unrecognizable. But I would never forget Paulie's face.

After they finished digging, Dante removed a gun from his holster. He aimed at Paulie while Nico, Angelo, and I pointed at the other pieces of shit.

"Any last words?" Dante asked.

Everyone but Paulie kept their eyes on the ground and waited for their imminent deaths.

"Salvatore deserved what he got," Paulie shouted. "He's the reason Giulia is dead."

"Don't you dare speak my mother's name," Dante snapped.

"It's true." Paulie inched closer to Dante, standing in the shallow grave. "I was close with your mother. Much closer than any of you ever realized. Sal's incompetence got her killed."

"You turned on my father because of an accident?"

Dante stood over Paulie and put the gun's tip to his forehead. "The bullet meant for him hit her instead. My dad had nothing to do with that."

"I loved Giulia." Paulie's voice shook as he spoke. "And your dad treated her like trash. Flaunted his relationship with Cara in front of her. She was going to leave him for me."

"The fuck she was." Dante smacked him on the side of the head with the gun. "Stop telling lies about the dead."

"That bullet should have hit Sal," he said with certainty. "I should know. I hired the hitman."

My heart sank into my stomach.

What the fuck?

Dante's usual expressionless mask slipped, and he emptied an entire clip into Paulie. He threw the gun at Paulie's dead body and spat in his grave.

I followed suit.

So did my brothers.

Pop, pop, pop.

Like a domino effect, all three men fell backward and into the pit.

"Do you think it's true?" Angelo asked Dante. "What Paulie said about Mom."

He shook his head. "No. Ma was a saint. She didn't have an affair with Paulie."

His words said one thing, but his face said another.

I didn't know my mother well. She died when I was eleven. But I remembered her hanging around with Paulie, even when my dad wasn't home.

I didn't think much of it back then.

Dante would never admit that our mother was anything other than a saint. That was how he chose to view her.

Paulie's confession was the truth.

Chapter Twenty

AVA

Dante held my hand as the doctor strolled into the room with an open chart, scanning the paper inside. He shut the door behind him and peeked at me with a tiny smile. "Ava, I have good news for you." Dr. Carter pulled out a chair from the counter and sat at my side. "You're carrying a healthy baby. We will continue to monitor both of you, but I don't see any cause for concern."

Dante squeezed my hand tighter and smiled, a real one that lit up his face. He did that a lot more now that I was about to marry him and carrying a Luciano baby. This morning, he said the baby and me gave him hope that all the shitty parts of our lives could produce something wonderful.

It was hard to believe that after everything we had

been through, we could have a happily ever after. Or at least the closest to one we would ever get.

After the doctor left the room, Dante pressed his palm to my stomach. It was too early to tell. We had to wait a few more weeks to find out the sex of the baby. It would be a surprise which of my guys fathered the child. They didn't want to know, anyway. To them, this baby, and any future children, would be Lucianos.

Dante leaned in to plant a kiss on my lips, the passion behind it making my head spin. When our lips separated, I was breathless.

"Take me home," I muttered. "I'm starving and need to rest."

He smirked. "Anything for my queen."

In the waiting room, we found Angelo, Stefan, and Nico. They had just as much of a right as Dante to be in the room with me. But for appearances, we agreed it was best to let Dante act as if he was the father. We already had enough attention on our family and didn't need anymore.

Nico rushed over to us, worry furrowing his brows. "What did the doctor say?"

"We're okay." I ran a hand over my stomach and smiled. "The drugs Johnny's guys fed me did no permanent damage."

He breathed a sigh of relief, staring down at my

belly. Angelo and Stefan also looked like the weight on their shoulders had disappeared instantly.

"Let's go home." I smiled at each of them. "We have a wedding to plan."

On the night of our engagement dinner, my stomach was a mess. Despite my fear, they all seemed happy about the new addition to the family. They wanted a big family, and none of my guys even cared who fathered the child.

We would raise them as a Luciano.

That was all that mattered to them.

I heard Dante's shoes tap on the hardwood floor in the hallway. Seconds later, he entered our bathroom. He'd moved all of my stuff into his apartment while I was still sleeping this morning. I never thought I would see Dante change for anyone—especially not for me. But he was taking our engagement and his new role within the family seriously.

Dante was all-in.

And all mine.

He entered the bathroom and put his hands on my shoulders, staring at me in the mirror. We didn't speak, just looked at each other. Dante swiped a loose curl and fastened it into one of the diamond hair pins he bought me.

He looked gorgeous and dressed in a black suit that clung to his muscular body like a glove. Too tempting for words.

He cupped my shoulders, eyes fixed on me. "You look beautiful." His fingers trailed down the length of my arm, leaving fire in his wake. "I'm a lucky man."

I smiled at his words. "Yes, you are, Mr. Luciano."

His hand skated down my neck and dipped between my breasts. Loving the feeling of his skin touching mine, I leaned back against his chest and breathed in his manly scent.

Dante buried his face in my neck and kissed my skin. "Your family just arrived."

"It still feels weird to call them that."

He shoved the hair off my shoulder. "The Vitales are your family, Ava."

"Angelo said he will tolerate Carlo and Joey for me. But I know it must be killing all of you after hating the Vitales for years."

His hands dropped from my body, and I instantly missed the loss of his touch. "This is what our father wanted."

I spun around to face him, putting my hands on my

hips. "You don't have to marry me because of your dad."

He inched toward me, pushing my back into the counter. "I'm marrying you because I want to spend the rest of my life with you. Because I can't stand the thought of anyone else getting the privilege of having you in their bed, by their side." Dante dipped his head down and sucked my bottom lip into his mouth. "You're mine, Ava." My heart beat so fast it felt like it was about to break through my chest. "If I didn't want to marry you, I would have given you to my brothers."

"Technically, you have."

He shook his head. "You know what I mean. Stop trying to find reasons why we don't make sense."

"I'm not."

Dante shoved a hand through his hair and sighed. "All week, you've been second-guessing everything. Why?"

I considered his question for a moment. If Bella had asked me the same question, I knew what I would tell her. So I decided to give him the truth.

"Because I don't feel worthy of you."

He stepped back, staring at me hard, and then he broke the silence by laughing. "Are you fucking serious?"

"Hey!" I swatted my hand at him and missed. "Don't laugh at me."

Dante surprised me by getting on his knees in front of me. Raising my hand to his mouth, he kissed my skin. His gaze moved to the massive diamond ring and then to my face. "Baby, I don't feel worthy of you."

"I never thought I would see Dante Luciano on his knees." A smile tugged at my mouth. "What a sight."

"Don't mock me, woman." He dropped my hand and rose to his full height. "You're smart. Beautiful. A pain in my ass. But you're perfect for me. You challenge me in ways no one ever has."

He kissed me so hard it drained the air from my lungs. It didn't last long, but it was enough to set my skin on fire.

"I'm glad you asked me to marry you."

His eyebrows rose. "Yeah?"

I nodded. "When I was a girl, I thought you were a god."

He laughed. "I'm just a man, baby."

"I would watch you at parties and see how people gravitated to you. You may not like people, but they like you. There's something about you, Dante." Hooking my arms around his neck, I smiled. "I don't know how to explain it. But I've always been drawn to you."

"I thought you had a crush on Nico."

"I had a crush on all four of you." I brushed my lips against his. "But you scared me the most."

"I'm a lot older than you," he pointed out. "When I was a man, you were still a girl. The twins are closer to your age than Nico and me."

"Angelo kinda scared me," I confessed. "He's always had that crazy look in his eyes. Stefan looked so sweet but still had that hard stare all of you have."

"I don't stare hard," he countered with a smirk.

"You have no idea how scary you four look when you're not talking or smiling. It's intimidating."

He pressed his lips together, and a worried expression darkened his handsome features.

"What's wrong?"

Dante turned on his heels and exited the bathroom, speaking with his back to me. "Nothing. Let's go. Your family is waiting."

"What are you not telling me, Dante?"

He stopped at the center of our bedroom, his body angled toward me. "The Vitales' men found Giancarlo."

I took a deep breath and blew it out my nose. For a while, I had been trying to prepare myself for the day they found my dad. Even though he wasn't my father biologically, he raised me. I still felt something for him, even after he screwed me over and stole my money.

"But you promised not to hurt him." I inched closer to Dante. "What are you going to do to him?"

He rolled his broad shoulders. "It's up to Vincenzo Vitale. Giancarlo owes him a lot of money."

I tugged on his jacket sleeve to stop him from walking away. "Dante, please. Let him go. I will work it off. I will do anything. You have to make a deal with Vincenzo."

He stopped moving, head turned away from me. "You're pregnant with a Luciano baby. Forget about working. You never have to work again. This isn't your responsibility, Ava."

"But I like working," I shot back. "I'm not going to sit in the apartment and be the perfect stay-at-home Mafia wife just because we're married."

His eyes met mine. "You want to continue laundering our money?"

I bobbed my head. "It's part of the family business. And I'm going to be a Luciano."

"Fine. You'll continue to work with me. But I won't allow you to work off Giancarlo's debts. That's not on you."

I put my palms on his chest and stared up at him. "Please, Dante. Let him live. Send him away. I will never ask you for anything ever again."

"If this is what you want..." His eyes met mine. "Fine. But you'll never see Giancarlo again."

I nodded. "I understand."

His lips pressed into a thin line. "I'll speak with Vincenzo after dinner."

I smiled so wide my cheeks burned. "Thank you."

"C'mon." He grabbed my hand. "Our guests are waiting for us."

Chapter Twenty-One

AVA

My private bridal suite was a hot mess. Bella tore through every rack in the store, adding dresses to the oversized ottoman at the center of the room until they spilled onto the floor.

"What are you doing?" I put my hands on my hips and stared at her in awe. "Stefan already picked out your bridesmaid dress."

Bella flicked her hair over her shoulder and chuckled. "I'm not wearing any of these to your wedding. Just trying them on for fun."

I cocked an eyebrow at her. "Then, what are you doing?"

"Do you remember prom dress shopping?" Bella sat in the oversized chair and draped her feet over the side. "We have to take some pics for Insta."

"No." I shook my head. "This is different. And Dante is a very private man. He'll be pissed if we post pics online."

"He's in the news every week." She gave me a pouty face and rose from the chair. "If he were so private, he would do a better job of staying off the grid."

"His dad just died," I pointed out. "Salvatore was a local celebrity. And with the casino going through major changes, he's in the spotlight more than normal. But our wedding is personal. Trust me. Dante won't like this."

I knew he would hate every idea that popped into my best friend's head.

Until her engagement to Pete Morelli, my friend posted her entire life online. Her dad didn't mind as long as she kept his name out of it. She mainly updated her feeds with pretty pictures, nothing that could get anyone in trouble. But I always keep my personal life out of the media's view. The less people knew about my life, the better.

My dad trained me from an early age that we were different from other people. I was only allowed to communicate with associates of the Lucianos. So I had no personal life apart from my friendship with Bella. I never had any long-term relationships.

"Yeah, whatever, bitch." Bella laughed as she

reached into her purse for her cell phone. "Try on your dress." She pointed at my gown. "At least let me take a pic for my camera roll. I promise not to share it."

I held up my hand. "No, not until the wedding."

Bella plopped down in the chair across from mine and lifted the champagne flutes, raising them in the air. "You're no fun. Drink with me."

Raising a glass of champagne to my lips, the smell turned my stomach. I turned my head away from the scent and pushed down the bile rising from my stomach. I hadn't told Bella about my pregnancy yet.

"What's wrong?"

"The smell." I set the glass on the table beside me, no longer wanting to hide the truth from her. "I'm pregnant."

"Holy shit!" Bella shot up from the chair and downed the rest of her glass. "You're preggers?" She put the empty glass on the table and tucked her long, black hair behind her ears. "Which one is the father?"

"I have no idea." Gulping down the sickness wreaking havoc on my stomach, I covered my mouth with my hand. "And I forgot to mention something else. Vittoria is coming today."

"Are you kidding me?" Bella flashed an annoyed look at me. "How many ways can you spell awkward? You fucked her ex-fiance on the floor of his apartment while she watched."

I blushed at the memory. "Yeah, well... She's my half-sister. So I asked her to be in the bridal party. I thought we should get to know each other since we'll be part of each other's lives."

A few minutes later, Vittoria entered the bridal suite in a navy blue wrap dress. Her black hair was frizzy and all over the place. I was thankful I had my mother's hair and her good looks. The Vitale genes didn't pass to me.

"Thanks for coming." I closed the distance between us. "It means a lot to me that you're here."

She forced a smile that made it more obvious her red lipstick was uneven. "I'm not going to like you overnight. Not after everything you put me through. But for the sake of our family, I'm willing to give you another chance."

Vittoria extended her hand for me to shake, but instead, I pulled her into a hug. My emotions were all over the place with my pregnancy hormones. She tensed at first and then relaxed in my arms after a moment, patting me on the back with her palm.

"I'm glad you're here. I always wanted a sister."

She stepped out of my embrace, a genuine smile on her lips. "Me too."

Chapter Twenty-Two

AVA

It was my wedding day. Nerves stirred in my belly, but my best friend was here to calm me down.

Bella stood behind me, her eyes meeting mine in the mirror. "You look beautiful, Ava." She brushed the hair off my shoulder and smiled. "The perfect Mafia bride."

I spun around and pulled her into a hug. "Can you believe I'm marrying Dante Luciano?"

Bella flicked her black hair over her shoulder, the curls spilling down her back, and smiled. "Girl, you have no idea the jealousy I'm feeling right now. Remember when we were kids, and we would talk about what it would be like to kiss one of the Luciano brothers?" I nodded, and she added, "And you get all of them. You're one lucky bitch."

"I had the biggest crush on Nico," I admitted. "There was something about the sadness in his eyes that drew me to him. I felt he would understand me the most, and I was right."

"But you're marrying Dante." She whistled. "That man would kill a woman with one look. He's intense."

"Dante's not as bad as he seems," I said in his defense. "And he's an animal in bed." I laughed at the thought of our first time together. "He broke my bed when he finally fucked me."

She burst into a fit of laughter. "Are you kidding?"

"Nope." I shook my head. "Even after the bed broke, he didn't stop. He's a savage."

Bella's eyes widened. "Damn, girl. Way to make your bestie jealous. You get to marry the boss. And I have to marry Pietro Morelli."

"Pete's a nice guy. He's fun, too. Likes to party. If you stop acting like the perfect Mafia wife and show him the real you, I think the two of you will get along just fine."

"You think so?"

I nodded. "I know so."

Bella stepped back to appraise my wedding gown. It was a custom dress Stefan helped the designer create for me. In this dress, I felt like the Boardwalk Queen.

A smirk graced Bella's pink glossed lips. "You look hot, girl." Her eyes widened at the massive cleavage I had on display. "Dante will pop a major boner when he sees you."

I snorted with laughter. "Dante isn't a teenage boy. That man has more control than anyone I've ever met. Trust me, he'll make it through the ceremony without tearing off my dress."

The wedding coordinator entered the room. "Ladies, you're on in five."

"We're ready," I told her.

Bella extended her hand to me and wiggled her fingertips. "You ready to get married, bestie?"

It was one of the most important days in my life, but I was still scared. Marrying Dante would put a massive target on my back. But I tried not to think about the downside of marrying the boss of the Boardwalk Mafia.

I loved Dante.

And his brothers.

I gripped Bella's hand as we stepped into the hallway. My skin was so slick with sweat I lost my grip on her hand. But she wiped our palms on her dress and didn't say a word.

When we stopped in front of the chapel doors, my throat closed up. Our families were Catholic, so they insisted on a Catholic wedding mass before the reception at the Portofino.

I turned to look at Bella, breathing harder, and covered my heart with my hand.

She dropped my hand and reached into the purse tucked under her arm. "Do you need your inhaler?"

"No." I blew out a deep breath. "It's just nerves. This feeling will go away."

The doors cracked open as the wedding planner walked through them. She beamed a bright smile at me, her eyes traveling up and down the length of my gown, but she didn't speak.

I could see Dante and his brothers at the end of the long aisle. They looked so sexy, dressed in black tuxedos. Our guests were already inside, waiting for me to make my grand entrance. All of the local Mafia families were in attendance. Even some of Dante's relatives from Sicily flew in on short notice for the special day.

The Lucianos were Mafia through and through. Their mother was from Sicily, the daughter of the boss. She was sent to America to marry Salvatore.

Among the crowd, I spotted Angelina and Enzo. They were the closest thing I had to family. After I learned the truth about my birth father, I also discovered I had a family.

Vincenzo knew I was his daughter and sent Angelina to work for my family. Angelina was a Vitale before she married Enzo. I was spending holidays and birthdays with my aunt and uncle all this time and didn't even know.

The doors flew open once more to start the bridal procession. Bella walked down the aisle to Italian orchestra music.

Then Vincenzo appeared beside me, and I latched onto his arm. He wasn't around for most of my life, but he insisted he give me away.

"You're a vision," he said with a smile. "Beautiful."

I smiled. "Thank you."

As we strolled down the aisle, I felt like royalty. The train was so long that it dragged halfway down the aisle behind me. Everyone smiled, stared, and even snapped pictures. I passed some of the most powerful men in the country. Men who could make or break careers.

The Lucianos weren't just Mafia.

They were like celebrities because of their casino. I noticed a lot of familiar faces, men who ran Fortune 500 companies, politicians, and even a few Hollywood celebrities.

I couldn't take my eyes off Dante when we stopped at the front of the church. Dante was so damn hand-some, his muscles bulging beneath the tuxedo. He gelled his dark hair to keep it off his forehead and was clean-shaven. His eyelashes were so long and black that they brushed his tanned skin when he blinked.

His lips parted as he appraised every inch of my body. Like he was internally stripping me bare. I couldn't wait until later for my sexy savage to come out and play.

I glanced at his brothers, who stood beside him, burning a hole through me with their gazes. How lucky was I? Not only did I get to marry Dante, but I got to keep all of them.

My father offered my hand to Dante, and a spark pricked my skin when we touched. I wondered if he felt it because I saw a flicker of acknowledgment in his golden-brown eyes.

"*Sei bellissima mia regina,*" Dante said as he slipped his fingers between mine, his breath on my earlobe sending a shiver down my spine.

You look beautiful, my queen.

I smiled at his words.

As the priest went through the motions of the ceremony, I gripped Dante's hand. And when it was time to exchange our wedding vows, Dante slid a platinum band of diamonds onto my finger. It matched my engagement ring perfectly, the diamonds shimmering when the light hit them.

We didn't write special vows, only repeated what the priest told us to say. The priest finished the ceremony with the nuptial blessing and a final prayer. A kiss was not part of a Catholic wedding. So when

Dante hooked his arm around me and crushed my lips with a kiss, I could hardly catch my breath.

Our tongues tangled, fighting possession over the other. Dante held me like he feared I would disappear if he let go. When our lips finally parted, I gazed into his eyes, breathing hard. Dante stared at me as if seeing me for the first time and brushed the pad of his thumb across my cheek.

He whispered, "*Mia brava ragazza.*"

My good girl.

After the ceremony, we returned to Portofino to prepare for the wedding reception. It still didn't feel real that I married Dante Luciano, of all people.

He dressed in a black tuxedo that molded to his muscular body, paired with a black bowtie. I stood in front of the mirror on the dining room wall and fixed my hair into place, glancing at him in the mirror.

Dante looked good enough to eat.

He stuffed his hands into his pockets, his eyes moving over each curve of my body. "Are you done fussing over yourself, Mrs. Luciano? We can't be late for our party."

I smiled at him in the mirror. "I'm still not used to that."

His eyebrows rose. "What?"

"My married name."

"You'll get used to it, Mrs. Luciano."

Dante extended his hand and then led me out of the apartment.

"What about your brothers?"

He hit the button on the wall to call the elevator. "They're meeting us downstairs." Once inside the car, he said, "For appearances, we have to maintain the illusion it's just you and I in this relationship."

"Sure, makes sense."

"No one can know that I share you with my brothers."

I leaned into his arm and glanced up at my delicious husband. "Of course not."

"Not even your friend."

"She already knows," I admitted. "I told her everything after the first time you touched me."

His jaw clenched, a disapproving look spreading across his face. "She's marrying Pete Morelli and knows better than to speak about our family. But no one else can know."

"I would never say anything," I shot back. "Not like I have any other friends. Why are you so worried about someone finding out?"

"We have a lot of enemies." He pressed his lips together, eyes on the doors as they opened onto the ground floor. "We can never be too careful."

"You forget I was born into this life, Dante."

My husband grabbed my hand and power walked down the long hallway, headed toward the casino as if he were on a mission. The reception didn't start for another hour. Our guests were having cocktails and hors d'oeuvres.

He pulled open the door to the ballroom, putting his hand on my lower back as he ushered me inside the massive room. Dozens of people were already here, with several hundred more expected within the hour.

Dante swiped champagne flutes from a server's tray and handed one to me. He dipped his head down, and his lips brushed my earlobe. "Don't leave my side tonight."

"I remember the days when you pretended to hate me. That wasn't that long ago." I smiled up at him. "Now, look at you. So protective of your wife."

"I never hated you, Ava." He clutched my chin with those golden-brown eyes searing through me. "I love you. If anyone were to touch you, I'd lose my fucking mind."

My eyebrows rose at his confession. "You love me?"

"Yes," he said through gritted teeth. "And don't go using my words against me."

"I would never." Smiling, I grabbed his tie and kissed his lips. "Because I love you, too, Dante."

Chapter Twenty-Three

ANGELO

Despite how our family made money, we blended with the titans of industry and politicians who gathered here tonight. Our father had the foresight to make us appear more legitimate in the eyes of the community. But people still knew what kind of men lurked beneath our designer suits.

Criminals.

Made men.

The men in this room didn't give a fuck as long as they got something out of us. Fear was a powerful motivator—something we used to our advantage.

Servers walked past us with trays of champagne and fluffy-looking pastries. I waved them off, too busy gawking at our girl. Ava latched onto Dante's arm like a pretty ornament.

The perfect Mafia wife.

She smiled and laughed, looking like sin in a white strapless dress. After the wedding ceremony, she swapped out the elaborate gown with a long train for a shorter, sexier dress Stefan picked for the event. Wearing the diamond tiara that Dante bought for Ava as something new, she looked like the Boardwalk Queen.

Our queen.

She may have married Dante, but she was ours. Turning every head, Ava strolled through the room with Dante. For once, he didn't look constipated. He was always so uptight, with a stick up his ass. But surprisingly, Dante seemed happy.

Content.

Some might even say he was smiling or something close to it. Ava had that effect on all of us.

Even me.

I could feel my walls crumble from the first time she touched my scar. It was like someone saw me for the first time in my life. She didn't care about the ugly scar or the fact it made me sick to my stomach each time I looked at myself in the mirror. I never felt ugly or unloved by her.

She made me feel whole again.

Ava grabbed popped a tiny pastry into her mouth and washed it down with a sip of water.

"She looks like a goddess," Stefan commented, leaning against my arm, with his eyes on Ava. "What the fuck did we do right to get her?"

I nodded. "Even Dante is coming around." I drank the rest of my scotch and set the glass on the table. "Look at him. He's different with her."

"Dante can deny it all he wants, but he's in love with her."

He never brought a date to our father's events. Even Stefan and I had taken girls from our clubs as arm candy to parties. Nico had girlfriends and dates over the years. He was the most normal of us.

But not Dante.

This was a first.

A married man.

When Ava glanced around the room once more, her eyes met mine. Her teeth grazed her bottom lip, which she frequently bit when nervous.

I rose from the chair and lowered my voice. "Dante's had her for long enough."

Stefan was at my side. "Agreed."

We left the table and headed straight for our girl. Her dark hair covered her breasts, pushed up in the tight dress that hugged her curves.

I wanted to rip the fabric to pieces with my bare hands like a savage. She fueled the carnal hunger inside me. Her innocence spoke to my darkness, and I wanted to smother her with it.

"Hey," she cooed. "Where have you guys been hiding?"

"In plain sight." I winked. "Come with us."

She turned her head to look at Dante, then back to us. "I'm not allowed to leave your brother's side. He gave me strict instructions."

My eyes narrowed at her. "The fuck you're not." I tapped Dante on the arm and leaned in to speak closer to his ear. "We're taking Ava off your hands for a little bit."

"Excuse me," he said to the senator he was talking to and then gritted his teeth at me. "No games or bull-shit," he said in a low, menacing tone. "If my wife comes back looking like she crawled out of an alley, we will have a problem."

"We'll take good care of our girl." I slapped him on the back and smirked. "She'll come back good as new."

"I'll hold you to it," he fired back.

I steered her through the bustling ballroom with Stefan on her left.

"Where are we going?" Ava asked as we left the room.

"Somewhere private."

"Ooh, I like the sound of this." She beamed a smile

at me. "Dante has been keeping me under close watch tonight."

I opened the door to the bridal suite with a keycard and flicked on the lights. Once inside, I put my hands on Ava's waist and kissed her.

"Did you miss me, baby?"

She moaned against my lips, desire flaring in her eyes as she grabbed me over my pants. "I missed your big dick."

"Mmm… He missed you, too."

I'd been with plenty of beautiful women, but I never craved anyone like Ava. This woman had her hooks in me, and I wasn't letting her go.

I held her against my chest. "We need to be inside you."

Her gaze moved between us. "At the same time?"

"Fuck, baby." I licked my lips. "Don't tempt us."

"I've never done that before," she said with a cute smile.

"The next time you come to the club, I'll break you in." Lifting her feet off the floor, I hooked my arm around her and lowered her to the couch. "We need to prepare you for that."

"Angelo," she said in that sultry voice that made my cock harder.

Stefan put his knee on the cushion beside us and leaned over to suck her bottom lip into his mouth.

Then, he unzipped his pants and pulled out his cock. "Did you miss me, too, *bellezza*?"

We hadn't spent much time together this week. Not with Dante keeping Ava busy with the wedding planning.

"Yes," she moaned against his lips.

I shoved her dress up and parted her thighs. Ava was so desperate to fuck that she unzipped my pants and fisted my cock, rubbing the tip along her wet slit.

And as I pushed into her tight pussy, she cried out. I slammed into her, spreading her open with one quick thrust. Her eyes closed every time she felt all of my piercings, one after the other.

"Fuck, baby. I missed your pussy."

She pressed her lips together as I moved in and out of her, so she could feel the metal rubbing her inner walls. "Oh, Angelo."

As I fucked her, she took Stefan into her mouth. He worked his dick past her pretty glossed lips and choked her with it. She gripped the cushion and hummed on his cock.

"My pretty little cock slut," Stefan grunted as he brushed the hair out of her face. "You handle both of us so well, baby."

"Yeah, she does," I muttered.

I pushed down the top of her dress and massaged her breast, rolling my thumb over her nipples. Tiny bumps dotted her olive skin, spreading down her arms.

After Stefan came, she screamed our names, her orgasm shaking through me. We didn't have time to waste. Not with our guests down the hall. Dante would come looking for Ava if we took too long. So I quickened my pace, fucking her until we both came.

I collapsed on top of her and kissed her lips. "I fucking love you, woman."

A grin stretched across her mouth, and she cupped my right cheek, stroking her thumb over the scar. "I love you, too, Angelo."

As if on cue, my cell phone rang. Not even a second to catch my fucking breath. I groaned as I retrieved the phone from my pocket.

It was Dante.

"Yeah?"

"Where the fuck did you go?"

"Taking care of our girl."

A beat passed before he said, "On our fucking wedding day? Couldn't you wait until tonight? Get back here. Now!"

Then he hung up.

Ava leaned against the couch and peeked up at me. "Everything okay?"

"We have to go. Daddy Dante summoned us."

She giggled and hopped up from the couch. "We better not upset Daddy."

"Come here, baby." Stefan helped Ava fix her dress back into place, knowing way too much about fashion to be related to me. "Perfect. Dante can't complain."

"He'll find something to complain about," she said with laughter in her voice. "You know my husband."

"I do."

She moved between us and sighed. "I hope both of you know I didn't just marry Dante. I made the vows to him, but it was to all of you when I said them."

"We know." I hooked my arm around her. "You're Mrs. Luciano now. It doesn't matter which of us you married."

Chapter Twenty-Four

AVA

After the wedding reception ended, I went home with my kings. I was a married woman. It still didn't feel real to call myself Mrs. Luciano. For most of my life, I looked at the Luciano brothers as if they were gods. I thought they were untouchable, invincible. I also never thought I would ever have a chance with them.

Dante carried me over the threshold because he was old school like that. He had to do everything by the book. I laughed and smashed my face into his neck as he brought me upstairs with his brothers following.

No one spoke a word.

No one even breathed.

Dante set me on the bed like I was a delicate,

breakable thing. He stared down at me like I was the center of his world. All of my guys did. I let my gaze wander between them. From Stefan to Nico to Angelo.

I loved all of them in different ways.

"I want to tell all of you something." Licking my lips, I looked up at them. "Something I remember about each of you. I married Dante, but we're a family now."

Angelo smiled so wide that it made the scar on his right cheek more prominent. Stefan gave me one of his dreamy looks. Of course, Nico's grin split his face in half. He always looked at me like that. And Dante, he seared my skin with one of his deadly but sexy gazes.

"Nico, you were my first crush." I got on my knees on the mattress and touched his arm. "When I was in middle school, I wrote your name all over the insides of my books. You've always made me feel safe, and I love that about you."

Nico grabbed my hand and brought it to his mouth. "I love you, *passerotta*."

After he dropped my hand, I moved on to Stefan. "And Stefan, you made me feel comfortable from the moment I came to live at the casino. My first night in the apartment was terrifying. But you stood out on the balcony with me and screamed. Thank you for that."

He got on his knees in front of me and kissed my

lips. "I love you, *bellezza*. From that moment, I knew you were the one."

I slid across the bed and grabbed Angelo's hand. "Angelo, when I first moved here, you scared the shit out of me." I chuckled, shaking my head, and he snickered. "But there was something about you that drew me to you. I still can't pinpoint what it was, but we had an instant connection. You let me touch your scar. That was when I felt your walls come crumbling down for me. I love you, and I couldn't imagine my life without you in it."

Angelo sucked my bottom lip into his mouth. "I fucking love you, *dolcezza*." He licked the length of my cheek. "You're so sweet."

After I kissed him, I moved over to Dante. He was still staring at me like he wanted to devour me, his eyes wild with desire. I clutched his hand, saving my husband for last.

"Dante, we haven't always gotten along. And we definitely started on the wrong foot. But I've learned so much from you over the last few months. You've taught me things about myself and the world. I love you, and I'm glad I get to call you my husband."

He bent down to capture my face in his hands and gave me a kiss that stole the air from my lungs. "You'll always be my good girl." Dante spanked my ass. "But tonight, I'll leave my mark on you." He smirked. "Lay back, my queen. Your kings want to conquer you."

He helped me out of my dress and tossed it at Stefan. Nico got on his knees and stripped off my panties. One quick tear, and they were gone.

Nico spread my thighs with his big hands while Angelo's lips were on my inner thigh, planting hot kisses. Dante just watched, turned on by his brothers taking control. My skin sizzled from the heat of their breath, an incredible sensation that went straight to my toes.

Stefan and Dante watched their brothers with their hard cocks poking through their pants. Usually, Angelo and Stefan tag-teamed me, but tonight Angelo and Nico were working so well together. My guys were becoming a functional unit. Their love for me helped them to overcome years of issues.

I kept my gaze on them as I shoved my hands through Angelo and Nico's hair. My sexy kings kissed their way up my thighs. But when they reached my pussy, Angelo shoved Nico out of the way. He looked up at me with his lips parted and rolled his tongue over my clit.

Dante tugged on his tie, studying my face as if he were trying to commit it to memory. I could tell he enjoyed watching me get off, even when he wasn't the one making me come.

I screamed for them, gripping Angelo's short, black hair as an earth-shattering orgasm swept through me like a storm. After I came, Dante pushed my back to the mattress, holding my arms above my head. He parted my lips with his tongue, rough and with the same passion I craved, claiming his wife like he wanted to scorch my skin with his sinful touch.

Dante pushed inside me, breaking through my inner walls. He never took his time or treated me like some delicate flower. I liked this side of Dante. At least I knew what to expect and braced myself for the roughness.

Nico massaged my breast while Stefan's teeth pierced my nipple, tugging on it like an animal. My nipples were sore, but the pain turned to pleasure as he bit and sucked.

"Dante," I whispered and then moaned each of their names.

A shiver ripped through my body. And after I came for them, Dante was right behind me.

Angelo didn't waste a second.

Dante had barely rolled onto the mattress beside me before Angelo flipped me onto my stomach, so he could enter me from behind. He fucked me hard. Like he hadn't had his way with me during the wedding reception.

He never seemed to get enough of me.

Stefan moved to the bed in front of me. He tugged on my hair and pushed his cock past my lips. Angelo marked me with each thrust. And when his hand came down hard on my ass, I screamed. But it only took a few times before I begged him for more.

Stefan came first, coating my tongue moments before Angelo came inside me. Nico laid on his back next to me and reached over to pull me on top of him. I pressed my palms to his chest and rode him into the mattress. He lasted the longest of his brothers. With Nico, it always felt like a marathon.

And after I came several times for him, he spilled inside me. Nico curled his arm around me and dragged me to the mattress.

"I can get used to that," I breathed with laughter in my tone.

Dante rolled onto his side and slipped his hand between my thighs. "I'll never get enough of you, Mrs. Luciano."

His brothers grunted in agreement.

"Tomorrow, we'll find out the sex of the baby." I looked at each of them. "And pretty soon, we'll know which one of you is my baby daddy."

"Doesn't matter to me," Nico said.

"Same," Stefan agreed.

Angelo nodded.

Dante rubbed his hand over my stomach. "This baby is a Luciano. The next Boardwalk King."

"What if it's a girl?"

Dante's lips brushed mine. "Then she'll be a powerful queen like her mother."

Eighteen months later...

Ava was sleeping with Angelo and Stefan when I cracked open the bedroom door. I was out later than usual with Nico, dealing with a dispute. Over the past year, Nico was becoming someone I leaned on. Someone I trusted.

And a good advisor.

"We should let them sleep," Nico whispered.

I shook my head. "No, I haven't seen Ava for more than an hour over the past two days. I'm sleeping next to my wife."

Nico tipped my head down the hall, a smile on his face. "I'm going to check on Salvatore."

Some days, I couldn't stand sharing my wife with

my brothers. But for the most part, this fucked-up relationship worked.

All of us moved into one apartment. Mine was larger than the others, so I broke through the wall of our father's apartment. Now we had more rooms than we could count.

Enough space for our growing family.

Ava delivered Salvatore last year. He was blond-haired with blue eyes.

Salvatore was Nico's son.

She got pregnant again a few months after she had him. Boy or girl, it didn't matter to me. But this time, she was carrying my child.

I made sure of it.

It was hard enough trying to explain why my son looked like Nico. So I told my brothers they could pull out or get the fuck out.

Nico headed down the hall to check on Salvatore. I shut the door behind me and sat on the edge of the bed, kicking off my shoes. Ava rolled over and stretched her arm across the empty space on the mattress.

"Dante?" She swept her arm to the right and brushed my thigh. "What time is it?"

"After two in the morning."

She groaned. "Again?"

I stripped off my clothes, rolled onto my side, and wrapped my arm around her. Ava was naked and rubbing her pussy on my cock. After the night I had, I wasn't ready to sleep. I wanted to fuck until I could forget every problem in my life. My wife was the only person who could take my mind off all the shit that haunted me.

"I missed you," I whispered right before I kissed her.

She moaned into my mouth when I cupped her breast in my hand. I rolled the pad of my thumb over her nipple, and the tiny bud hardened.

I couldn't see her face in the darkness, but I didn't need to see Ava to feel her. I knew every curve of her body, every imperfection, every scar. Her hips were wider, and her breasts fuller with this baby.

I loved her new body.

Sometimes, Ava was self-conscious about her new figure, but I couldn't get enough of her. She was beautiful, perfect in every way.

I moved my hand down her stomach and between her legs. She was wet for me, rocking her hips into my hand. I slid two fingers inside her, long enough to feel how much I turned her on. Pulling down her bottom lip, I rubbed her juices along her skin and made her suck on my fingers.

I reached between us with my other hand and

fisted my cock, teasing her for a second before I moved her on top of me and inched inside her.

"Mmm…" Ava rode me, pressing her palms to my chest. "Dante, I missed you, too."

No matter how much she hated my late nights and the dirty shit I did for my family, Ava forgave me for all my sins in the bedroom. I needed her forgiveness, needed her to absolve me of my sins.

She was my salvation.

I moved my hand up to her chin, forced her to look me in the eyes, and then fucked her even harder. Her moans turned into screams that woke up Angelo. Stefan was out cold, his back facing us.

Angelo sat up and watched us for a moment, scrubbing at his tired eyes with his hand. He moved behind Ava and gripped her hips. "You're so fucking sexy." He massaged her breasts, breathing on her cheek. "I love seeing you pregnant again with our baby."

She grabbed his hand and sucked on his fingers like they were his cock, muffling her moans as I ripped an orgasm from her body. Angelo bent down and tugged at her flesh with his teeth.

I slammed into her even harder, losing myself with Ava. She gave herself to me fully, and I wanted to take everything she had to offer.

In the bedroom, she was what I needed her to be, what she wanted to be for me. Outside of these walls, I lived my life one day at a time, hoping to make it to the next. But with Ava, I could wash away my guilt and forget about the past. We were lost in each other, too consumed to stop. Even after I came, I kept going, my cock still hard inside her and greedy for more.

Angelo ran his palm over her ass and dropped to the bed on her other side. The twins had her to themselves all night. He knew better than to get in the way and didn't try to fuck her.

I only had a few hours until I had to get back to work. The casino was in the process of major renovations. We were also building a second tower for our hotel guests. Add in the usual Mafia drama, and I was lucky if I got three hours of sleep.

Ava slid off me and rested her hand over my heart. "How was your day?"

"Too long." I kissed her on the forehead and hugged her tighter. "I missed you and Salvatore. I hate spending this much time away from the two of you."

"Then don't," she whispered. "Hire someone to handle the hotel and casino."

I let out a frustrated sigh. "This isn't a normal job. You know that. I don't keep business hours."

"Dinner tonight. Be there." Ava kissed my lips. "I don't care if the casino is on fire. You're making your mother's gnocchi for us."

"Whatever you want, Boss."

Her nose touched mine. "I love you."

I fisted her hair and brought her lips to mine. "I love you, too."

I took her bottom lip in my mouth and sucked on it. She opened wider, granting me the access I needed. With each flick of our tongues, I could block out everything I'd done that day.

Every sin I'd ever committed.

Once our lips separated, we stared into each other's eyes, breathing heavily. I pushed her back to the mattress and pinned her down with my body, spreading her legs open to make room for me. My cock was hard again and had a mind of its own. But, unlike last time, I didn't wait for her body to relax.

Digging my fingers into her thighs, I threw them over my shoulders and slammed into her. She turned her head to the side to kiss Angelo, then her eyes were back on me.

"You must be sorry for missing dinner," Ava bit out with a sexy smile on her lips. "Oh, Dante. Fuck me."

With each thrust, Ava looked up at me, her eyes full of pure ecstasy, and yelled for me to keep going. My girl loved it rough, and I loved giving it to her.

"I killed someone today," I confessed.

I told Ava everything.

We had no secrets.

"Yeah," she moaned. "Why did you do it?"

"Because he was planning to rat out our family to the police."

Ava reached up to push her hands into my chest as if forcing me off her when she only wanted me to fight her. She loved the push and pull. I lived for the nights when she wanted me this way.

"How did you do it?" Her breathing intensified, chest rising and falling as she got closer to her release. "Tell me everything, Dante."

"Two shots to the head."

With her clenched around my cock, I closed my eyes and hissed from the sensation which rocked through my body. My legs shook, and I spilled my cum inside her seconds later.

"Damn," she whispered, still out of breath, when I collapsed on top of her. "That was…"

The sweat from my forehead mixed with hers as I kissed her. "Therapeutic."

She giggled. "That's one word for it."

Angelo leaned over and kissed her. "I'll kill every fucking person in this city if you fuck me like that, *dolcezza*."

Ava tapped his bicep with her hand and laughed. "Don't you dare."

He shoved his hand between her thighs to spread her wider. "Then open up for me. My dick is harder than steel from watching you with Dante."

"You like watching the boss fuck me?" Ava clicked her tongue. "Huh?"

"Baby, you have no idea." After I moved to the mattress, he lined himself up at her entrance and grunted once inside her. "Fuck."

"Are you guys ever going to stop fucking?" Stefan rolled over with the pillow covering the side of his face. "I'm trying to sleep."

"Since when do you choose sleep over pussy?" Angelo joked as he fucked Ava like an animal. "Our queen is so wet. You don't know what you're missing."

Stefan put the pillow behind his head and sighed. "I love fucking Ava. But until Salvatore starts sleeping through the night, I'll take any sleep I can get."

I laid my head on the pillow, with her hair in my face and the smell of her shampoo filling my nostrils. My eyelids fluttered, fighting sleep. Most nights, I awoke from nightmares of my mother's death. Some nights it was my father. But waking up with Ava by my side seemed to make everything better.

I stared at my beautiful wife and rubbed her clit as she came for Angelo. Feeling left out, Stefan massaged her big tits. She was seven months pregnant with my son and more beautiful than ever.

After Angelo came, still inside her, he moved his hand to her belly. "You're having my baby next."

"Fuck you," Stefan snapped. "I'm older. I get the next baby."

"Both of you," I interjected before this turned into a fight, "shut the fuck up. Or get the fuck out. We're not talking about this now."

I heard Salvatore crying from the hallway, his voice getting louder as Nico moved closer to my bedroom and opened the door. He stood in the entryway, rocking him on his shoulder.

Nico stepped into the room and handed the baby to Ava. "I think he's hungry."

When we discovered we were having a boy, we couldn't agree on a name. Ava chose Salvatore in honor of our father, and we loved her even more for it.

She fed the baby and brushed her fingers through his thin blond hair. Nico sat on the bed beside me and smiled. He never felt like he was part of the family until Ava came into our lives. Our girl helped heal some of the old wounds and brought us together.

Salvatore passed out in Ava's arms.

None of us spoke a word.

We just looked at Ava and our son.

She rubbed her palm over her baby bump and winced. "He's kicking me." Then she clutched my hand and placed it on her stomach, so I could feel our son moving inside her. "I have a feeling Antonio is going to be a handful."

"If he's anything like his dad," Angelo commented, "he'll be ordering us around in no time."

I smirked. "You wouldn't know how to function without me leading this family.

He paused for a beat and then nodded.

My brothers relied on my leadership.

Ava reached out for our hands and laid them on her stomach. A big smile stretched across her face. "We're creating the next generation. One day, our sons will be the Kings of the Boardwalk."

Meet the Salvatore brothers and the Queen of The Devil's Knights.

Learn more about the series at JillianFrost.com

Get to know Jillian Frost

Watch Jillian's latest videos on TikTok
@jillianfrostbooks

Get sneak peeks and an all-access pass to Jillian on
Facebook when you join her private reader's group
called Frost's Fangirls

Check out the latest teasers and pretty pictures on
Jillian's Instagram @jillianfrostbooks

About the Author

Jillian Frost is a dark romance author who believes even the villain deserves a happily ever after. When she's not plotting all the ways to disrupt the lives of her characters, you can usually find Jillian by the pool, soaking up the Florida sunshine.

Learn more about Jillian's books at JillianFrost.com